THE STOLEN PLANS MYSTERY

THE STOLEN·PLANS· MYSTERY

by
NORVIN
PALLAS

WILDSIDE PRESS

CHAPTER 1

LULU

The signpost said, "Forestdale, 20 miles," the first time their home town had been mentioned, and Ted Wilford and Nelson Morgan felt a tingling of anticipation. After a strenuous three months at college, they were more than ready for, if not exactly a rest, at least something a little different.

"Until I'm actually home, I feel as if that college is chasing me," Nelson commented, while keeping his eye carefully on the road. "I can almost feel its hot breath on my neck."

"I thought you liked college," Ted returned, sniffing at the air. Maybe it was just his imagination, but it was even beginning to *smell* like home.

"Oh, I liked it all right, but it was a pretty steady grind. You get behind at college, and they don't fool around with you. You're just *out.* And if I'd been tossed out of college, it would just about have killed me."

"Oh, come on, get off it," Ted objected. He knew that Nelson wasn't likely to be expelled as long as he was willing to give his books as much attention as he did the gridiron.

"Sure it would, because then I'd have to go to *work.* Well, anyway, I brought home half a trunk load of textbooks, and you know something? I might even look at some of them. But I didn't notice you bringing much, Ted."

"No, I'm traveling light. I'm caught up with everything, and I imagine I can find something around the house in case I get overcome with an irresistible urge to study. Anyway—"

"Anyway, there's Lulu," Nelson concluded with a grin, for he had read Ted's last letter from home.

"Well, there's no reason why I shouldn't at least meet her," Ted defended himself. "Just as a courtesy I'll have to drop in and see Mr.

Dobson at the *Town Crier* office, and I suppose if Lulu's around he'll have to introduce me."

"Sure he will, and just in case he overlooks it, you'll hang around until he does. Well, I'd do the same thing in your place. Your mother made her sound pretty attractive."

"Yes, I know," said Ted, frowning. "Mom said she knew I'd be anxious to get acquainted. Now what makes her think that? She knows I don't go chasing after every girl I see."

"This Lulu must be pretty special. Your mother ought to know."

"Maybe, but special in what way? If Mom wanted to arouse my curiosity, she sure knew how to do it. Anyway, I wonder why Mr. Dobson wanted to take another girl on? I didn't think they were that busy."

"Must be Lulu's specialty," Nelson reminded him, but since he knew no more about Lulu than Ted did, the discussion ground to a halt.

Still, Ted could not help wondering just what his mother had meant. He had written back and asked some carefully worded questions, but in her next letter his mother hadn't mentioned Lulu at all. Maybe that had been her way of getting back at him for being a little slow about writing home once or twice. Well, they were nearing the outskirts of Forestdale, and probably quite soon he would meet Lulu, and find out what this was all about.

The remaining miles sped by. They topped the last crest before Forestdale, and the little town came into view.

"Well, there she is," Nelson remarked with some pride, as though he had discovered the place himself.

"I wonder if we'll find things changed very much."

"Say, we've only been gone three months. I don't think Forestdale would change very much even in a hundred years, except for the people—and sometimes I'm not even sure about them."

"Look," said Ted tentatively, "I don't see why you should bother dropping me off at home."

Nelson gave him a swift glance of amazement. "I only live about two or three minutes away from your place—as the engine goes— remember?"

"I know, but I was just thinking. Mom won't be home till evening anyway, so why should I sit around alone in an empty house? We'll be going right past the *Town Crier* office, so—"

"So you might as well stop in and see Lulu. Well, if you promise to introduce me to Lulu the first chance you get, I'll drop you anywhere you please. You sure anybody'll be at the *Town Crier* this time of day?"

The office was supposed to close at noon on Saturdays, but somehow this deadline was seldom observed. Ted had grown to like Saturday afternoons at the newspaper office. The printer had gone home so that the linotype in the rear was still; the telephone jangled a little less often than usual; and sometimes no one at all dropped in.

"Probably Mr. Dobson'll be there. I think sometimes he likes to just sit there by himself, even if he doesn't have anything to do. We'll know by the light."

Nelson maneuvered the car into a parking space, then got out to get Ted's suitcase from the trunk. The office was brightly lighted, and through the frost-covered pane they could see someone sitting at a desk. Ted felt that he was really home at last. He took his suitcase from Nelson's grasp.

"Thanks, Nel. I'll call you tonight."

"Sure, and if you don't I will," said Nelson with emphasis. He drove off.

At the sound of the door opening, Mr. Dobson looked up. "Well, Ted!" He suddenly beamed, and came around the front of the desk, extending his hand. "College must agree with you. You're looking fine."

"You, too, Mr. Dobson," Ted returned, putting his suitcase on the floor and shaking hands.

"Well, come on, Ted, sit down. Your mother told you I wanted to see you, I suppose?"

"Not exactly." Things were becoming a little clearer to Ted now. His mother hadn't told him to call on Mr. Dobson. She had just mentioned Lulu, and relied on his curiosity to do the rest—and of course she would have told him later if it didn't. Anyway, there was no one else in the office just then—that much was certain. Maybe there wasn't any girl named Lulu after all.

Ted moved his suitcase out of the way and sat down. The office seemed a little smaller than he remembered it, and he was soon able to account for some of the difference. In front of the big plate-glass window there was a stack of something under a canvas cover. Probably some advertising literature that had overflowed from the printing room, Ted decided, for the *Town Crier* occasionally did some job printing as well. It made the whole room seem crowded.

"Anyway, I did want to see you. How would you like to work here during your vacation, Ted? If you have anything else planned, then that's perfectly all right. But if you don't feel too tired or too busy, then I could use you."

"That sounds as if it would be a lot of fun, Mr. Dobson," said Ted slowly, "only—"

"Carl Allison will be gone over the holidays," the editor went right on. "Carl's been doing some good work, and I think he's getting the feeling that he really belongs. I hope I'm not giving away any secrets when I tell you that he's found a girl in whom he is very much interested, and I wouldn't be surprised if they were to announce their engagement soon. Carl is such a cautious person that I don't believe he would take such a step unless he felt he had a permanent business connection. I told him plainly that I was satisfied with him, if he was satisfied to be here. Since then he's been almost like a changed person."

As long as Mr. Dobson really needed him, and as long as there wasn't going to be any trouble with Carl, Ted had no further objections, and his voice became enthusiastic.

"Just what will you want me to do, Mr. Dobson?"

"In general, make yourself useful around the office, the way you always have. But you'll have a few of Carl's regular jobs, too. You'll check the police blotter every day—"

The police blotter! This was something he had long looked forward to. While it was true that he had been more or less loosely associated with the *Town Crier* before, he had never been called upon to check the police blotter.

Mr. Dobson was going on, telling about the hospital, the fire station, and other places Ted would have to call. Though Ted was listening, he was also thinking that this was going to be a much better vacation than he had planned. He felt that the spirit of Christmas was hanging in the air. He was even willing to believe that Carl Allison had—well, maybe not exactly changed, but at least become less belligerent. Anyway, right then Ted felt that he wasn't mad at anybody.

When Mr. Dobson had finished, Ted remarked, "How soon do you want me to start?"

"Oh, there's nothing more doing today, Ted. You can start Monday. Actually there won't be as much doing as usual next week. People read less than usual just before Christmas. Advertisers know it, and seldom bother pushing anything except gifts. Public officials know it, and they don't bother giving their usual interviews and publicity releases. I'm afraid our paper is going to be rather skimpy for the next couple of weeks, except for the Christmas advertising, and that's mostly in already."

"Yes, I knew things would be a little slack. That's why I wondered why you needed an extra girl. My mother wrote to me about Lulu."

"Oh, did she?" Mr. Dobson smiled. "But evidently she didn't mention that we needed Lulu for our promotion."

"What sort of promotion is it?" asked Ted.

"Well, it's a contest. The *Town Crier* is sponsoring it, in cooperation with eighteen of the small merchants in town. It's been running for two weeks already. Next week is the last."

Ted was puzzled. "I thought you didn't care much for contests, Mr. Dobson."

"Oh, I certainly don't object to contests as such, Ted. I just think it's very difficult to get exactly the right kind. If your contest is too hard, few people enter it. If it's too easy, you run into a great many ties. Another thing is that there are always a great many more losers than winners, and this often leaves an atmosphere of ill will. I think this is especially true where the selection of winners depends a good deal upon judgment or opinion. In any essay contest, for instance, most of the losers will probably feel that their essay was just as good as the winner's. But finally Mr. Markum, who's running the contest for us, came up with an idea which seemed to answer most of these objections. He was able to line up a sufficient number of merchants, so I decided to let the newspaper play along. The first prize is a thousand dollars, and there are lesser prizes as well."

A thousand dollars was a good-sized prize for a local competition, Ted thought. It might seem like small potatoes, compared to the big prizes often given away on television, but, on the other hand, a person's chance of winning here was much greater, too.

"How does the contest work?" asked Ted, curious to know how all of Mr. Dobson's objections could be met.

"Well, the contest depends upon a window display. It's in each merchant's window on a different day. The display consists of exactly twenty objects. On each succeeding day, one object is changed. That is, it may be, but on some days the display is exactly the same as it was the day before. That's for the contestant to decide. If an object has been changed, the contestant must tell what object was removed and what was substituted in its place. The promoter assured me that there won't be very many ties. It's a contest simple enough for anyone to enter, but not many people will end up with a perfect score."

It sounded like a novel idea, but Ted was not convinced of its effectiveness. "I shouldn't think it would be too hard, Mr. Dobson. Why not simply take a list of the twenty objects, and then the next day check them off one by one?"

"I'm afraid it isn't that easy, Ted. It would be simpler if the object substituted were of a completely different kind. But it won't be. For example, a red teapot might be removed and a pink teapot substituted. Or a slightly larger box might be substituted for a smaller one. And of course the arrangement of the items will be completely different. This contest will be a real test of a person's powers of observation."

This did seem to make for an interesting contest, but Ted quickly thought of a further objection. "What would stop a person from taking a picture of each display and comparing the pictures?"

"That is one hazard, Ted, and the contest specifically says that anyone taking pictures will be barred. Furthermore, we keep a sort of watch over the display, and the display is withdrawn as soon as the store closes—for of course the real purpose is to draw people into the stores. But Mr. Markum has convinced me that anyone who relies solely on a camera will be caught. There are a few subtle traps—such as the fact that a camera will not be able to tell accurately the size of an object where the distance cannot be closely measured. It will be up to Lulu to detect cheating of this sort."

"Oh, is that what Lulu is going to do?" asked Ted.

"Yes, Ted, Lulu is going to take over the judging of the contest." He walked over toward the front window. "Ted, I want you to meet Lulu."

CHAPTER 2

A COOL RECEPTION

Ted looked around. He thought possibly Lulu had come into the room quietly while they were talking, but apparently she hadn't. They were still alone.

The editor had removed the canvas cover from what Ted had thought was a stack of circulars. Now he saw that he had been completely mistaken. What lay uncovered was a substantial piece of machinery of some sort. It was about half as large as a piano, and worked by electricity, for there was a cord trailing to the nearest outlet. As Mr. Dobson turned on the switch, various lights began to flash through the front openings.

"What is it?" asked Ted curiously.

"This, Ted, is an electronic brain. It's not one of the largest ones, of course. In fact, it has probably been superseded by more advanced models. But still it can do an amazing number of things. This is what I mean by grading the contestants' answers impartially. People will hardly be able to resent it if Lulu here picks out the winners. Of course it is true that Lulu can do only the things we tell her to do, and it may be that we could judge the entries by hand faster than by telling Lulu how to do it. Still, it's an interesting gimmick. Mr. Markum gives a demonstration every morning, and usually quite a crowd of people gathers outside the window to watch him."

"But how does it work?"

Mr. Dobson smiled. "I'm out of my depth there, Ted. You'll have to watch one of Mr. Markum's demonstrations, and I'm sure he'll be able to answer your questions."

Though Ted had no idea what the machine was doing just then, it certainly was an impressive sight. He wondered if the flashing lights in front had any real purpose, or whether they were there for mere window dressing. If it were not for the lights, a viewer would hardly know that the machine was in operation. As it was, one got the feeling that something very mysterious and important was going on.

Several passers-by had paused curiously. Mr. Dobson allowed the machine to run on for a few minutes, then switched it off and replaced the canvas cover.

Now that he knew Lulu was a piece of machinery rather than a flesh-and-blood girl, Ted could hardly tell whether he was disappointed or not. It might have been fun having a new girl around, but he knew plenty of girls in Forestdale, and Lulu aroused his scientific curiosity. He was looking forward to having a talk with Mr. Markum and learning more about this machine with human qualities.

"Yes, you do get the feeling that Lulu is almost a person," Mr. Dobson was saying, "especially after you hear Mr. Markum's explanations. It seems that each one of these machines has a personality of its own, just as people do. I don't think the losing contestants will get mad at our Lulu."

He leaned back in his chair, and remarked:

"You can go if you want to, Ted. I'm just waiting for Santa Claus."

Ted started to smile, then realized this was something more than a joke. "Santa Claus?"

"Yes. That is, Mr. Gentry. He's the Santa Claus at Kirtland's this year, and we've borrowed him for our promotion. He makes an appearance at each one of the stores on a separate afternoon—whichever store has the current display. Kirtland's, of course, is too large to be interested in this promotion, but Mr. Kirtland doesn't mind helping out smaller competitors. His motto is 'prosperity for each one means prosperity for all.' There is no particular reason why Mr. Gentry should stop in here after his day's work, but he likes to let us know how things have gone, and I suppose he likes to talk."

"Has Mr. Gentry always been the Santa Claus at Kirtland's?"

"No, he's new this year. Mr. Sanders, who's been there for many years, felt the job was getting to be too much for him. Mr. Gentry was a newcomer to town, and applied for a position of some sort. Then Mr. Kirtland decided he was just the type for Santa Claus. Very few people know Santa Claus's real identity. For some reason Mr. Kirtland feels it's best to conceal it."

"How does Mr. Gentry fit in with this contest?" asked Ted.

"Oh, he gives out small gifts to the children—Santa Claus books, balloons, and other small toys. These small merchants feel that if they can get the little children to come in, the mothers will have to come with them, and then, of course, the mothers may see something they want to purchase."

Ted decided that he had a little more time to kill, and might as well wait to see Santa Claus. Meanwhile, he could ask Mr. Dobson about what had been going on during his absence.

"Any more promotions, Mr. Dobson, aside from this contest?"

"Well, not exactly promotions. We had a safety campaign during the fall months, and among other things helped sponsor safety patrols in various schools. There's one item of unfinished business in connection with that. The papers in back of the program have planned a Christmas treat for the patrol leaders. That's next Saturday night—two days before Christmas. The party is going to be held in Jasonville, and we'll need someone to take a carload of youngsters there. I thought maybe you and Nelson might like the job. Of course we could ask one of the parents, but it is kind of a roundabout trip gathering them together, and it really seems to me that the newspaper ought to furnish the transportation. As a Y camp leader, Nelson ought to be able to keep order without spoiling the boys' fun."

"Yes, I think he'd go along with that all right," Ted agreed. "What about Christmas turkeys? Is the *Town Crier* giving them away again this year?"

"Oh, yes, we'll be giving out our usual supply. But they can be delivered earlier on Saturday. You may get that job, too, Ted."

"That's all right with me. I expected to work, only that doesn't sound much like work."

"Here's something else, Ted, if you haven't happened to see a recent copy of the *Town Crier.* This year we're running a feature called 'Make a Wish.' You know that no matter how prosperous times are, there are always some people who are hard hit financially, due to illness or other misfortune. As a general thing the welfare organizations are able to provide for these people."

Or if they don't, they soon hear about it from Mr. Dobson, Ted thought.

"But sometimes that doesn't seem quite enough, especially at Christmas. These people are human, and often they have some little wish that would make their fives so much happier if it could be granted. Usually it doesn't cost very much, but still it's more than they can meet out of welfare allowances. The *Town Crier* prints these stories—carefully safeguarding all names involved—and readers are invited to contribute the item which has been asked for. We've had a very good response to our appeals so far. I believe there is only one request that has gone unanswered, and sometimes we have a whole flood of offers. I think something like that makes the whole town feel more of the spirit of Christmas."

As though in answer to these words, the "spirit of Christmas," as personified by Santa Claus, came in the door just then. He was carrying a sack over his back from which a number of toys protruded.

"Ted, this is Mr. Gentry," Mr. Dobson said.

Ted shook hands with the still-masked Santa Claus.

"The face looks familiar," Ted remarked with a grin. "I think we've met before."

"Anyway, I hope we have, Ted," Mr. Gentry returned, "in spirit, if not in person."

"How did things go today?" Mr. Dobson questioned.

"Oh, very well, very well. We had a fine turnout. I ran out of snappers and had to send out for more. I was afraid I was going to run out of Santa Claus books, too, but fortunately I didn't. I'll need a new supply, though."

"Ted, they're stacked back in the printing room. Would you like to put a couple of bundles in Mr. Gentry's car?"

"Sure thing," Ted agreed.

In the back room he switched on the light, and found the books lined up against the wall. After carrying two unopened bundles out to the car in front of the office, he returned to the office and found the two men talking. He decided this was a convenient time to take his leave.

"I'll be in Monday morning, Mr. Dobson. And I'll see you on Christmas Eve, Santa Claus."

"Well, now, I hope so, Ted, but I'll have to study your record first," and on this note Ted left them.

Ted, walking slowly, looked about him. Window displays had been changed, and there were Christmas decorations everywhere, but other than that he saw no evidence that things were different than they had been when he had left.

At home he found his mother had not yet arrived, and he let himself in with his own key. The house was comfortably warm, and everything was just as he remembered it, except that nothing seemed to be *out* of place, as there surely would have been if he or his brother Ronald had been home. He decided he might as well get his things put away, and took his suitcase upstairs. He discovered that his room had been newly painted, saving him a job he had expected to have to do over the holidays. Soon he heard the front door open, and ran downstairs.

"Ted!" His mother carefully put down all her bundles before coming to greet him.

"Hi, Mom. Everything looks great. What's in that big package?"

"Now, now, let's not be too nosy. Did you have a nice trip?"

"Oh, yes, we made good time. I stopped off to see Mr. Dobson, and I'm going to be working—I guess you knew that. And I saw Lulu, too. I know this was just a joke of yours, but hereafter I promise I'll write home every week, and if nothing exciting happens I'll make something up."

With a smile his mother took a contest entry card from her purse and showed him how she had filled it out up until that day. Because of Ted's relationship to the paper, she was not eligible for the contest, but she was trying her luck with it just the same.

"How about today?" Ted inquired.

"Well, I'm not sure, Ted. There's a vase that seems to be shaped a little differently from the way I remember it. But I spoke with Mrs. Talbert, and she seems to think it was the pillow—only I had that listed yesterday."

"Then a lot of people are interested in the contest?" asked Ted, more concerned about that angle.

"Oh, yes, Ted. Nearly everyone I know is entering."

"And Lulu—is that helping, too?"

"Yes, I think so, Ted. For one thing it interests the men, who might otherwise not want to bother with the contest. Oh, Lulu is some girl—just as I told you in my letters."

They had a pleasant supper. Ted remarked upon his newly-painted room and the new telephone extension he had noticed upstairs.

"In a way it seemed a little bit silly," his mother explained. "There aren't so many calls with you and Ronald away. But when you were home there was usually someone downstairs to answer the phone, and now very often there isn't. I've got plug-in phones, so we can have a phone in any room we please, and disconnect it in the bedroom at night, if we want to."

To this Ted replied that he thought it was a good idea. Not long afterward the phone rang. It was Nelson. He had already found out all about Lulu, but he didn't mind kidding Ted a little.

After Nelson had hung up, Ted read the evening paper, finally unpacked his clothes, and then, remembering all the things he still had planned for the holidays, wondered if this might not be a good time to catch Ken Kutler, his old friend and rival on the North Ridge *News-Record,* at home. He hated to bother Ken at the office if it wasn't necessary, and he knew Ken would be expecting to hear from him. He dialed Ken's number.

"Yes?" It was Ken's wife who answered.

"Mrs. Kutler, this is Ted Wilford."

"Ted? Oh, yes." Her voice sounded restrained and a little cautious.

"Does Ken happen to be anywhere around?"

"I'm sorry, Ted, but he isn't here just now."

"Oh, I see. I didn't want anything special, but if he gets a chance I'd like to have him call me."

"All right, Ted. I'm sure he'll call you if he can. I'm sorry now, but I think I hear the baby crying. Good-by," and she hung up quite abruptly.

Ted couldn't help but believe that Mrs. Kutler had been very anxious to get rid of him. Since she had always been friendly enough toward him before, Ted was puzzled by her attitude. Something else she had said sounded strange, too. She said Ken would call him if he could. Why wouldn't Ken be able to call in the next week or two?

"Mom, is Ken sick or anything?"

"No, I don't think so. I noticed that he had a signed article in the last issue of the *News-Record"*

But if Ken wasn't there and might not be able to call, it could mean only one thing: he must be off somewhere. And his wife was anxious to avoid talking with Ted for fear she might give something away. Ted began to feel uneasy, for he knew that Ken was always most dangerous when you didn't know what he was up to. His uneasiness grew upon him as Ken did not return his call that evening nor on Sunday.

CHAPTER 3

THE POLICE BLOTTER

Monday morning found Ted looking forward eagerly to work. Though he had been a familiar figure around the *Town Crier* for a long time, beginning in the days when his elder brother Ronald had held the position now held by Carl Allison, checking the police blotter was a new and challenging task.

At the office he renewed his acquaintance with the secretary, Miss Monroe, then waited for his instructions from Mr. Dobson. Monday morning was always a busy time, for the deadline for Tuesday morning's issue came at noon, and there was usually a last-minute flurry. The editor showed Ted the dummy on which the stories already set up in type had been mounted, and indicated a blank space of about half a column reserved for police, fire, and hospital news.

"That's the first thing to take care of, Ted. Bring that back as soon as you can. Do you want to take my car?"

"Not this time, Mr. Dobson, everything's so close together, but ask me again. I'll be back before you miss me."

At the station he found Sergeant Jeffers on duty. The sergeant knew of his past association with the paper, and did not for a moment question his right to be there. Ted felt more assured and mature, but what the sergeant had for him came as a complete letdown.

"Not very much here, I'm afraid, Ted. It's been a quiet weekend. Just two traffic arrests, other than parking tickets, and Mr. Dobson doesn't bother about those unless they start mounting up."

Ted dutifully wrote down the names and details of the traffic offenders, printing the names in big block letters to avoid any likelihood of mistakes. As part of the *Town Crier's* continuing safety campaign, Mr. Dobson always printed this information. He then noticed an additional entry on the blotter—not a bank robbery, but at least some petty stealing. He asked for further details.

"Oh, that. Just a few items of merchandise missing from one of the stores. We always run into that sort of thing, especially during the heavy shopping season. Sometimes I have my doubts that the stuff was really stolen. It could easily get mislaid or broken, when they're so busy. But they notify us anyway, just on the chance it might turn up."

"Have you been getting much of this lately?"

"Oh, yes. Seems there's a new report almost every day. But that's nothing unusual. We've had other years almost as bad as this."

"Have you recovered any of the merchandise?"

"Well, no." The sergeant seemed almost apologetic. "But then, they never give us much to go on. Any steady offender we'd get on to. But this is just casual, petty stuff, and, as I said, sometimes I doubt that it was really taken at all."

"What stores have reported thefts lately?"

Sergeant Jeffers ran off a list of names, until he came to Kirtland's, the town's largest department store. Ted knew that Kirtland's had its own private detective. Surely the store wouldn't have reported a theft to the police unless it was sure.

"What was taken from Kirtland's?"

The sergeant flipped back several pages. "Let's see, a little girl's doll stroller, a tricycle, a Chinese puzzle set, and some smaller things. Imagine walking out of a store with a tricycle hidden under your coat! Either somebody wasn't on the ball, or else it never really happened."

It did sound rather ridiculous. And it did seem like a funny sort of thing to steal. Knowing Kirtland's, Ted thought it would have been much easier for a thief to walk off with something like jewelry, which would be both smaller and more valuable. Though Ted felt they were really thefts, the value of the items was not very great. He decided to write down the details, and leave it to Mr. Dobson to decide whether or not to use the material. He thanked the sergeant, and left the station.

The hospital was his next call. A couple of new citizens had come into the world, but Ted knew this was outside his field. Miss Monroe would pick up that information by telephoning the Bureau of Vital Statistics. Ted looked over the list on hospital admittances, found nothing there he felt he could use, and left the building.

He was lucky enough to find the fire chief himself available at the firehouse, and he, too, did not ask to see Ted's credentials.

"Only one alarm since Allison was in last, Ted. It wasn't serious, as it turned out, but it might have been. Asphyxiation. It seems that you simply can't teach people not to try to heat a room with their cooking stoves and burners. That's something to watch out for at this time of year. I hope we don't have any real tragedies before the winter's over."

"I thought there isn't much danger of carbon monoxide, as long as there's a flue connected."

"Well, a flue helps, of course, though sometimes even these get clogged up, especially if they are too small. But carbon monoxide isn't the only danger. In a small, closed room the burners may simply use up all the oxygen. A person gets sleepy and headachy and groggy before he realizes what has happened. Strangely enough, accidents like these seem to be on the increase, in spite of all we can do to warn people."

"Why is that?" asked Ted with interest.

"One thing is that rooms tend to be smaller than they used to in the old days. Another is storm windows—they help keep the rooms nice and warm, but if you board yourself up too well, where's the fresh air going to come from? Another thing is migrations. A lot of people are moving up from the South, and though it seems odd to us here, they've never had much experience with heating their rooms before, especially through a cold winter."

Ted began to see the possibility of a story. Mr. Dobson was a bug on safety, and traffic safety wasn't the only kind, was it? He asked for further details on the recent case, and wrote them down.

Returning to the office, he gave Mr. Dobson the information he had picked up. As Sergeant Jeffers had predicted, the editor wasn't much impressed by the missing merchandise.

"He's right, Ted. That sort of thing is commonplace. The stores and the police do the best they can with it, and as long as the values involved are small, there doesn't seem much point in dwelling on it. Of course if the thefts should continue after the holiday season, and a kind of pattern to them develops, then it would be a different matter. But this asphyxiation business is something else. We've printed warnings before, but it seems you need a new one every year. Better get to your typewriter, Ted, and write it up. Try to quote the fire chief as much as possible, if you can remember his words."

Ted moved thankfully over to the desk. On his first day at the paper he was really writing a story. He had written other stories before, but the thrill never quite left him. The thoughts that he—Ted Wilford—was now putting down on paper were going to be read by thousands of people. It was like giving a speech before a large and attentive audience.

For the next twenty minutes Ted's typewriter keys clacked. When he was finished he knew he didn't have a masterpiece (who could write a masterpiece with a clock in front of him ominously counting off the minutes?) but he did have a workmanlike job completed.

He took the story to Mr. Dobson who read it over, made a couple of minor changes, then felt obliged to cross out a whole paragraph as he estimated the space available. He nodded his approval, and Ted took his story back to the printing room.

There were tasks in the office to keep Ted busy, but altogether it turned out to be fairly quiet for a Monday morning. The deadline was easily beaten, and the presses started to roll before twelve o'clock.

With the paper on the presses, for better or for worse, everyone in the office relaxed a little. Even if there were mistakes—and careful as they were it seemed that some small ones nearly always crept in—there was nothing that could be done about them now, and so they might as well not worry about them.

"What will you want me to do this afternoon?" Ted inquired of Mr. Dobson.

"I wish I had an assignment for you, Ted, but I'm afraid I don't. This is the quiet season of the year, as far as news stories go, so I can't even promise you that the next couple of weeks will be any more exciting. There's plenty of routine work to do around the office, though. I'm sure Miss Monroe can use some assistance with the mail."

"What about Lulu?" asked Ted, for the electronic brain was sitting quietly under its canvas cover.

"Oh, yes, Ted. Mr. Markum will be in at noon. If you want to catch his demonstration, perhaps you could go out and have your lunch now."

This seemed like a good idea to Ted, and he managed to return to the office just as the noon whistles were blowing. Mr. Markum was already there, Lulu was uncovered, and the tubes were flashing. Andy Markum was only a few years older than Ted, and within a few minutes they were using first names.

A small group had gathered outside the window—women among them, Ted was interested to note. Andy had large placards on which problems were printed. Ted read the first one:

> A man has a mortgage of $7,833 on his house. His interest rate is 5½ per cent, and he pays at the rate of $76.00 per month. How many months will it take him to pay off his mortgage?

Andy used an auxiliary machine to punch a few holes into a card, fed the card into the big machine, and within less than a minute Lulu printed an answer on a paper, which Andy copied on a large blackboard and held up for the audience outside to see. He followed with other problems.

During this demonstration Ted felt a growing respect and admiration for Andy. It was true that Lulu was doing the actual calculating, but it was Andy who was feeding the information to the machine. In doing that he had to know a good deal about mathematical principles as well as the machine's method of operating. Maybe Lulu was a big brain, but the person who could master and direct Lulu was no slouch, either.

"Can this machine do simple addition?" one of the onlookers who had come inside inquired.

"Yes," Andy returned, smiling, "but what's the use? Would you ask a man like Einstein to add a column of figures which you could do just as easily yourself on an adding machine? Actually there would be very little timesaving on problems like that. Although Lulu calculates like lightning, the delays involved in feeding the information into the machine and waiting for the answer to be printed would make such a demonstration unimpressive.

"Lulu is at her best in demonstrating roots and powers. Suppose you wanted to carry 65 to the 65th power. That would take you all day—if you didn't make a mistake. Lulu can do it in a fraction of a second. Of course you could work the problem by using tables of logarithms. On this mortgage problem, for example, if you gave an answer to the nearest full month that would be accurate enough, since the man pays only once a month anyway. But many scientific problems need a more accurate answer than logarithmic tables will give them."

"But does this machine work on the same principle as an adding machine?" asked another.

"No, I wouldn't say that. An adding machine has to have nine different keys. All Lulu has is tubes, which may or may not light up. This is called a digital system. One tube unlighted would be zero. One tube lighted up would be 1. One tube on and one tube off would be 2. Two tubes on would be 3. One tube on and two off would be 4, and so on. We can represent all the numbers simply with tubes. This system gives Lulu considerable speed and flexibility which an adding machine doesn't have."

"You call this machine a big brain. Just how does it compare with a human brain?"

"That depends on which function of the human brain you're talking about. Lulu has speed. She can do problems in a few seconds which would actually take a person years and years to calculate by himself. She wins out in accuracy, too. Lulu simply doesn't make mistakes, if she is hooked up properly and the information fed to her in the proper way. There is even a check on burned-out tubes. Another function is memory. Lulu's memory is limited, but as far as it goes it is completely accurate. Lulu doesn't forget anything until we tell her to."

"Well, I wish I had a memory like that when it came to taking a history exam," remarked Nelson, who had just joined them.

"I wonder. Would you really want a memory that remembered all the unimportant things in the same way as the important things? Before you had gone very far that way, you'd begin to wish you could forget a few things."

"Now that leaves me with a good argument for my history professor," Nelson decided. "I'll tell him the stuff wasn't important enough to make an impression on my brain."

"This brings us up to Lulu's three important limitations. One is capacity. The largest electronic brain ever built has only a small fraction of the capacity of the human brain. The brain has billions of cells, but where would we put billions of tubes, even if we had them?

"Another limitation is judgment. Lulu has no judgment extending beyond the judgment of the builder and operator of the machine. Should you carry an umbrella today? Lulu can't tell you. Maybe someday we'll have a machine that will tell you whether it's going to rain, but how much the rain is going to bother you is a matter for your own judgment.

"And finally there is creative imagination. Lulu has nothing like that. She can't imagine a situation that has never existed before."

With the demonstration over, the crowd dispersed. Ted helped Andy cover up the machine and gather his effects together.

"You're a college man, aren't you?" asked Ted.

"Two years at Interstate Tech," said Andy, almost curtly. This was one of the leading engineering colleges in the country. "Then my money gave out."

"Couldn't you have qualified for a scholarship?"

"The competition is pretty stiff. A few top men qualified, but I didn't. The college is in a small town, too, so there aren't any jobs."

"I know." Ted nodded. "It's the same thing at my college—Oakland. But you're going back, aren't you?"

Andy shrugged. "I don't know. I'd like to. I could be designing these machines instead of just operating them. But when you get out working things seem a little different. If you're supporting yourself you never save as much money as you expect to, so it takes you longer. Something else changes, too. You feel that you're getting along all right, so why should you go back to the old rat race, grubbing over a nickel and pretending you're going to amount to something, when nobody else seems to care?"

His bitterness took Ted by surprise. It didn't seem to him that Andy had much of a problem. If he wanted to go back to college he could; if he didn't want to, he didn't have to. It seemed like a simple proposition—too simple to account for Andy's overwhelming bitterness.

CHAPTER 4

TED PLAYS SANTA CLAUS

After Andy had left the office, Ted settled down to helping Miss Monroe with the mail. Much of it was routine, and he was familiar enough with the procedure to know what to do with it. But there was one type of letter which was unusual as far as he was concerned.

"Miss Monroe, what are all these thank-you letters about, and how do you want me to handle them?"

"Oh, those, Ted. They're the aftermath of our Make a Wish program. A good many articles have come in, and we've distributed them to the persons for whom they were intended. Many of the recipients write letters of thanks, and of course they address them to the paper, since they don't know the names of the donors."

"Does Mr. Dobson want to publish any of these letters?"

"No, he's opposed to it on principle, although a good many other papers do print letters of that kind. He naturally wants to hide the names of the recipients, and as you know the *Town Crier* very seldom publishes unsigned letters. But there's another side of it, too. He is just as determined to keep the names and circumstances of the donors secret. He feels they should give for the sake of good will, and not for the sake of getting some publicity."

Ted laid the small pile of letters aside. "It seems a shame to waste these letters, though. You can tell how much these people mean it. Maybe the people making the donations would like to hear about it."

"They'll hear, Ted. We copy each of these letters, omitting signatures and anything else that might identify the writer, and send them on to the donors. And of course, after Christmas, Mr. Dobson will write an editorial thanking everyone who contributed."

Ted was given the task of retyping these letters, and just as he finished a telephone call came which relieved him of further clerical duties that day.

"That was good news, Miss Monroe," Mr. Dobson announced as he replaced the receiver. "It looks like Mary Jane is going to get her portable typewriter. It's been so long since we printed that item I was beginning to lose hope. I guess even used typewriters are in considerable demand. We had an offer of an upright," he explained to Ted, "but it wouldn't have done her much good, confined to bed as she is."

"Looks like Santa Claus made it just in time," Ted observed.

"Oh, Mary Jane was going to get her typewriter, all right, even if I had to beg, borrow, or steal it. Ted, how would you like to play Santa Claus—pick up the typewriter and deliver it to Mary Jane?"

"It's fine with me, Mr. Dobson."

"Here are my car keys. And oh, Ted, one thing—sometimes the people who offer to donate things do mean well, but the article they have to offer is really too battered up to make a suitable gift. If that should happen to be the case, decline it as tactfully as you can. And try to get back by four o'clock, as I'm due at an editors' dinner tonight in Horntown, and it's a long drive."

Picking up the slip of paper on which Mr. Dobson had written the two addresses he needed, Ted went out. As he drove along, he hoped that the typewriter would turn out to be very good, but if not that it would be very bad. If it were in between, he might have trouble deciding whether to take it or not. Fortunately for all concerned it developed that he had no problem at all, for the typewriter was a beautiful one.

His drive to Mary Jane's took Ted through the center of town. He drove slowly until he was hailed from the curb. It was Cliff Corby, an old friend on the high-school newspaper, whom Ted hadn't seen since September. He drew over to the curb.

"Well, how's it going? You're sure the sporty one. What did you do, rob a bank or something?"

"Oh, I'm pretending I'm working. Just delivering this typewriter for Mr. Dobson." He lifted the lid.

"Nobby," said Cliff, shifting his burdens to the other arm. "Oh, I bet I know—that's the typewriter someone asked for in the paper's Make a Wish column. Know something? I've got a can of polish at home that would shine that thing up so you couldn't tell it from new. You got time?"

Ted reflected that this was part of his job. "I guess so, come on." He opened the door, and Cliff climbed in.

When they reached his house, Cliff took Ted down to the basement to hunt for the polish.

"If I don't find it, you're going to think I was just mooching a ride," he said with a laugh. However, he found the can and set to work on the typewriter, refusing Ted's offer to help. "Not in that suit. Anyway, it won't take me long."

He was as good as his word, and the metal gradually took on a resplendent gleam. It really was almost as good as new.

"Say, Ted, what goes with Mr. Sawyer?" Cliff remarked as he was almost finished.

"Mr. Sawyer?" He was the new circulation manager for the *Town Crier*. Ted knew him only slightly, but had never heard any complaints about his work. "Nothing that I know of. What's the matter?"

"Can't say exactly. He lives right behind me, you know. He seems to be keeping all kinds of weird hours. The lights from his drive come right in my bedroom window, and sometimes they wake me up in the middle of the night with cars going in and out."

"He works all night at the *Town Crier* office—on Mondays and Thursdays."

"I know that, but what about the other nights? Anyway, I don't think it's his car. And what kind of visitors do you get in the middle of the night?"

"Maybe somebody working a late shift, just getting off duty."

"Well, maybe." Cliff shrugged. "But my dad happened to meet him the other day, and he was awfully cool and standoffish, as if he didn't want anybody asking him questions. My mother thought maybe there was some illness in the family."

"Not that I know of. Nobody at the office said anything to me."

Mr. Oliver, the former circulation manager, had left at about the time Ted entered college, and his place had been taken by Mr. Sawyer, a fairly new arrival in town. Since the *Town Crier* had no need for a full-time circulation manager, they were obliged to take a part-time man who also held some other job. Mr. Sawyer was employed as a salesman, but he was able to arrange his own hours so that he could handle the *Town Crier* work, too. Ted had heard that he was an ambitious young man, with a wife and two small children, who was glad of the extra work. He came to the office at night after the others had left, sent the papers on their way, and had gone home by the time the office opened the next morning. He worked in the same quiet and efficient way his predecessor had, so it was almost as if the work were being done by elves, as Mr. Dobson once suggested.

Since Ted had no explanation to offer for Mr. Sawyer's nocturnal visitations, Cliff did not pursue the subject, but continued with his polishing until he was fully satisfied. He held the typewriter up to the light.

"Swell," Ted assured him. "A certain person is going to be very well pleased with this."

"Male or female?"

Ted shook his head. "That would be telling."

Ten minutes later he was pulling up at Mary Jane's door. Both the bedridden girl and her mother were delighted with the typewriter.

As Ted left the house to return to the office, he felt a little glow inside. Playing Santa Claus *was* fun, and something everybody ought to try.

CHAPTER 5

THE POWER FAILURE

At five o'clock Ted, the last to leave the front office, went to the door of the back room to tell Mr. White, the printer, he was going. Then he left by the front entrance, locking the door behind him. It was twilight, with the heavily overcast sky cutting off even the few stray rays from a setting sun.

There was no particular rush for Ted to get home, since he knew his mother was shopping, and had planned a late supper. It seemed to Ted a good opportunity for him to take care of some of his own shopping while he had the chance. At Kirtland's he found Santa Claus was apparently going off duty, for this was the time of day when there would be few small children about. At the moment he was reentering the store for something he had forgotten earlier.

Ted said hello to him, and received a cordial nod in return without knowing whether Mr. Gentry remembered him or not among all the hundreds of people he saw each day. He was carrying a sack of toys as usual, even on his way home, for apparently he didn't want any children to see him without his toys, the most important thing to a child. Ted was not certain whether Mr. Gentry had been to the *Town Crier* office that day, though probably he had been there as usual, while Ted was out.

For more than an hour Ted wandered from one aisle to another, making a few purchases, but finding the whole process taking a good deal longer than he had planned. Any thought that he might complete all his shopping that evening had long since disappeared. He was beginning to grow tired and a little hungry, for he had had nothing except a candy bar since noon, and wondered whether he ought to give up for the time being.

Suddenly the lights grew dim and began to flicker. People stopped what they were doing and looked up toward the lighting fixtures. The lights held to their pale glow for the better part of a minute, and everyone was wondering if this was going to be all, or whether they were due to go out entirely. Some of the floorwalkers began scurrying about, while some of the customers started to leave hurriedly, not wishing to get caught in the large store in the dark. Except for this, nearly all noise had ceased as people waited to see what was going to happen.

The suspense ended as the lights flared brightly for an instant and then gradually faded into darkness, leaving an afterglow that lasted for some seconds longer before it, too, faded out. Then near pandemonium reigned. Friends who had been separated from each other called out, trying to locate each other in the dark. There was a general crowding toward the exits, with people bumping into each other and into the counters. A few people thought to take out cigarette lighters, and others took up the idea, until little glows of fight sparkled through the aisles. It was feeble enough, but much better than nothing. By this time some of the employees had returned with flashlights, and were trying to unscramble the traffic leading to the exits.

After a few minutes the lights came on again, dimly, and an announcement came over the public-address system.

"Ladies and gentlemen, this is Mr. Kirtland speaking. We regret that there has been a general power failure at the electric company. We have switched to our auxiliary generator, but as you can see the light is inadequate to conduct our regular business by. We ask that you do not attempt to make any further purchases just now, and save yourself from frustration and possible disappointment in your selections. As soon as power is restored, Kirtland's will be happy to give you the same kind of efficient and courteous service we have always tried to bring you in the past. Thank you very much for your patience and understanding."

Most of the people were now filing toward the exits. With his few purchases held securely in his arm, Ted joined the others leaving the building in an orderly fashion.

Outside the darkness seemed almost overwhelming, although auto headlights gave some illumination. Here and there a star broke through the cloud cover and seemed unusually bright, just as stars usually seem brighter in the country than in town. Few places had auxiliary generators as Kirtland's did, though Ted knew that the hospital and some other public buildings had emergency facilities. But most of the establishments were thrown back upon candles and a few spare flashlights. All over Forestdale business had come to a standstill. In the streets traffic was jammed up, for not only were the street lights out, but the traffic signals as well. Drivers motioned out the window to other drivers, but even so traffic was merely crawling along, and at some busy intersections it snarled completely. Ted knew that all available policemen would be called to emergency duty, but this would take awhile.

The *Town Crier* office—why, the power failure would stop the presses. This meant that Mr. White wasn't going to get done in time. Well, that was something that couldn't be helped. No doubt he would be willing to work overtime, but even that wouldn't help if the return of the power should be long delayed.

Thinking of the newspaper, Ted suddenly thought of something which hit him with stunning force. This was a newspaper story, wasn't it? It had one strong defect—there was nothing secret about it, so it lacked the element of surprise. But on the other side of the picture people liked to read a story about something they felt they themselves were involved in. It wasn't the sort of story that was likely to win a Pulitzer prize, but for a little town like Forestdale it was important. With Mr. Dobson and Carl Allison both out of town, who was there to cover the story except Ted?

What to do first? Ted thought of calling the power company to determine the cause and extent of the trouble, but decided against it. Whenever there was a power failure, people always flooded the company with calls needlessly, because the company had instruments which would tell them whenever any substantial portion of their service wasn't functioning. Ted doubted that his call would get through at all, and even if it did, he didn't care to add to the company's harassment at a moment when they were doubtless doing their best to restore service. He could check with the company later.

Then what, back to the office? He knew that when people were unable to get through to the power company, their next impulse was to call the newspaper. But Ted couldn't see much sense in sitting in a dark office and listening to complaints that he couldn't do anything about. No, he'd better get around and see what he could pick up— how people were reacting, how much trouble it was causing, perhaps a few human-interest stories. Then tomorrow he could check at the police station, firehouse, and hospital on his usual beat to see how their facilities had held up during the emergency.

Moving through the streets, watching the tie-up, listening to people's complaints, taking an occasional note, Ted began to appreciate how much electricity means to a modern city. When the electricity stops, nearly everything else stops. No business, little traffic flowing, everybody worried and excited. And what about people in their homes? There was very little to do except sit around and wait. No television, except for those few people with portable sets. He recalled that a good many homes had electrically controlled furnaces which would now be inoperative unless they also had a manual control. That meant there were hundreds of homes in Forestdale gradually cooling off. On a bitter winter night that could be serious if the failure was prolonged. Electric stoves meant no cooking.

What about refrigerators and freezers? If these defrosted, a good many householders were going to find their meat spoiled. But if this was true of people in homes, what about meat dealers like Mr. Compton? He could lose all the meat in his locker, possibly worth hundreds or thousands of dollars. Since the shop was only a few blocks away, Ted decided to walk over and see if anything was coming off.

As he turned the corner he saw Mr. Compton hurry into the store carrying a flashlight. By the time Ted reached the store, a minute or two later, Mr. Compton was coming out again. He locked the door, then looked up and recognized Ted.

"Oh, Ted, how are you? Back from college, I see. Like it?"

"Oh, yes, it was fine." But Ted was more interested in talking about Mr. Compton's problem. "Had to come back to protect your meat?"

"Yes, I started right over as soon as the lights went out. I'd hate to lose that big locker full of Christmas orders."

"Any chance that you will lose it?"

"That all depends on how long the power stays off. If it's only a matter of a few hours I'll be all right. But if the meat starts to thaw, I'm out of luck, except for what I can sell immediately. We aren't supposed to refreeze it. I'm insured, so I'm not worried about the money, but I hate to disappoint so many customers. It's hard to get rush replacement orders at this time of year."

"Would ice help you out any?"

"Regular ice? No. It's not cold enough. A lot of people try that in their home freezers, but the best thing they can do is simply to leave the cabinet closed. It's insulated, and the cold will last for a good while if they keep it shut. Of course, if the current doesn't come back for a long time, then they're out of luck anyway."

"What about dry ice?"

The butcher made a gesture with his hands. "Might help, but who's got a supply of dry ice on hand just when they need it? By the time I rustled around trying to get enough dry ice, either the power would be back on, or else it would be too late."

He walked over toward his car. "Can I give you a lift anywhere, Ted?"

"No, I'm just scouting around for the newspaper, seeing how the power failure is affecting everyone. That reminds me, you're in the *Town Crier's* window contest, aren't you?"

"Yes. My day is next Saturday."

"The last shopping day before Christmas? I should think you'd have your hands full then without bothering with Santa Claus."

"I will, Ted, but Santa Claus won't bother me much, and I want him there for a special purpose. You know I give out a few free turkeys to lucky customers, and I want Santa Claus to pull the winning tickets for me. Did Mr. Dobson speak to you about delivering Christmas turkeys?"

"Yes, he did. I'll be on hand Saturday to help out. See you then, Mr. Compton, if not before. Good night."

"Good night, Ted."

Ted returned to the center of the business district and made more notes. A few people, recognizing him and concluding that he was representing the newspaper, gave their opinions to him, and he wrote down a few of their comments for possible publication. Being without electricity in the middle of winter certainly did excite people. Meanwhile the whole life of the town depended upon the efforts of a few power workers and how fast they could locate and correct the trouble.

More than an hour after the failure the current suddenly came on again. Satisfied that there was nothing more for him to do, Ted headed toward home.

After supper had been cleared away, Ted decided to do a little work on his story. He couldn't finish it until he had spoken with the police tomorrow, but it would help if he had something to show Mr. Dobson besides his haphazard notes, probably illegible to anyone except himself. Perhaps it wouldn't hurt to call the power company. The emergency was over, and he might be able to get a satisfactory explanation from them now. He put through the call.

"This is Ted Wilford, calling for the *Town Crier.* Can you tell me what happened at the plant to cause the power failure?"

He was immediately switched to another line, and then to still another party, until at last a man's voice came on. When he had repeated the same statement for the third time, the man's voice became guarded. It wasn't that he objected to speaking to Ted, but knowing he was talking for publication, he wanted to be careful to say exactly what he meant.

"It was icing conditions, Ted, that broke one of our main feeder cables. We immediately switched to the auxiliary feeders, but they were unable to carry the additional load, and burned out. It was just one of those snafus that don't appear to be anybody's fault."

"The whole station was out, then?"

"Every blessed light that was served by our station. Our repairmen made good time, though. I'm going to congratulate them tomorrow."

The conversation continued for another couple of minutes, and then Ted thanked him and hung up. He had the man's name, but didn't know, until he checked the next day, that he had been speaking to the president himself!

He set about writing his story, which occupied him till nine o'clock, when the telephone rang. Ted answered.

"Hello, Ted?" He recognized at once that friendly but very casual voice. "This is Ken Kutler."

"Well, Ken. I'm glad you called. I tried to get in touch with you last Saturday, but I wasn't able to reach you."

"I know. My wife gave me your message, but I couldn't call before now."

"You were out of town, then?"

"Oh, no. On the contrary, I was very much *in* town. The truth is, Ted, that I'm in jail!"

CHAPTER 6

AN ALL-NIGHT JOB

At first, Ted's impression was that Ken must be joking. Then he recalled a few other things: Ken's absence and his delay in calling back, and Mrs. Kutler's coolness, and he knew that this was no joke. If Ken said he was in jail, then he really was in jail.

"What did they get you for *this* time?" Ted inquired.

"Overtime parking. They threw the book at me."

This much, at least, was a joke. Ted was thinking rapidly. He knew that Ken's deadlines were the same as his own, and that this could account for Ken's delay in calling until Monday night. Ken's story must be already in print, and would be out the next morning. Anything that Ken might say to Ted now would not help him if he tried to muscle in on Ken's story. Evidently Ken's reason for occupying a jail cell had something to do with a story. However, he did not inquire directly. If Ken wanted to tell about his story, it was up to him.

"I kind of thought they'd catch up with you someday," said Ted lightly. "How long are you in for?"

"Ten days, starting last Friday morning. Ten days is the usual sentence for a misdemeanor, you know, and so that's what I asked the judge for."

"You *asked* the judge?"

"Oh, yes. The newspaper's paying for my keep in jail, so why shouldn't I get things the way I want them? The funny thing is that there really is a law in this state that prisoners are supposed to pay for their own keep. Few people have heard about it, because it's very rarely enforced."

"Ten days—won't that carry you into Christmas?"

"Yes, Christmas morning. I didn't dare stay any longer than that, for even my ever-patient wife might explode if I wasn't home on Christmas morning to take pictures of our first born. By the way, she told me to be sure to apologize to you. She said she was scared to death when you called Saturday night. She hasn't known you very long, but she's already developed a healthy respect for the prowess of the Wilford brothers. Of course I may have exaggerated your exploits to her." This last spared Ted the embarrassment of replying to a compliment.

"Well, I suppose I'll be reading about it in tomorrow's *News-Record*."

"Oh, it's no great shakes as a story, Ted. Nothing startling about it—more seasonal and human interest. This is the slack time of year for news anyway—even worse than midsummer. So someone at our office—I assure you it wasn't I—got a brain wave and decided to send me to jail. How does a prisoner feel when he's facing a holiday season, knowing the whole world outside is celebrating? I didn't know before, but I'm getting a good inkling now. This gives me a chance to talk to prisoners confidentially, and weave in the background of their cases. Each story is a tragedy in its own way. I'm not getting *all* the answers, but I'm discovering some of the reasons why."

"I take it they don't know you're a newspaperman?"

"Oh, no, I'm a prisoner just like the rest. You ought to see my beard and my clothes. It might startle you—but then, again, maybe it wouldn't. You've already seen me in some of my more disreputable moments. And I even came equipped with a long case record of my past crimes—most of them untrue."

"It looks like you'll have material for a whole series of stories."

"Three stories—yes. Tomorrow, Friday, and then next Tuesday, the day after Christmas. That will enable me to carry the story right up to the preparation for Christmas dinner in jail—and it's better to let the readers imagine the rest. Of course I could carry the series indefinitely, but there's no use overdoing a good thing. Besides, I don't feel so easy about things, now that I know you're back in town. You're working down at the *Town Crier,* I suppose?"

"I'm a glorified office boy, if that's what you mean."

"I know. That's the way it usually starts, and then before I know what's happened you've got a story by the tail. You seem to have an affinity for news stories, and worse luck for me, you're one of those unusual persons who can recognize a news story when it happens—

it's surprising that most people can't, in its early stages. Ron was the same way. Is he getting home this season?"

"Yes, we're expecting him Sunday night, and he'll probably leave Wednesday morning."

"Then I'll have to get in touch with him sometime Tuesday. I don't suppose you're holding out on me, Ted—nothing big touched off while I've been incarcerated?"

"No, I don't think so," said Ted regretfully. "Just a few odds and ends."

"Well, I hope that's really true," said Ken dubiously. "I know you wouldn't tell me anyway, but I'm counting on the slack holiday season to keep you out of my hair."

"Meanwhile, you're picking up a pretty good story yourself," Ted reminded him.

"Well, maybe. The only thing I'm finding out for sure is that this a good place to stay out of."

He laughed, and with an exchange of holiday greetings they hung up. It occurred to Ted that having Ken out of circulation for a while might be quite a relief. He wouldn't have to spend every moment with the thought in the back of his head that maybe Ken was up to something.

He was about to turn on a television program when the telephone rang again. The caller was the *Town Crier's* printer who sounded very excited.

"Ted? White. Say, Ted, do you know what's happened to Mr. Sawyer?"

"Why, no." He glanced at the clock. It was well past nine o'clock, and Mr. Sawyer was usually on duty not later than eight. Of course the power failure had helped knock everybody off schedule. "He might still be in. Everybody's been delayed."

"Well, I haven't heard that the *trains* have been delayed, and we have to meet *their* schedule. It took me a couple of hours longer myself, with the power off, and I knew I couldn't get finished before he was due to show up. But I pushed right along, and by the time I was through and he still wasn't here, I began to get curious. I called him, but couldn't get an answer, so I drove out past his place and it was all dark. Mr. Dobson's out of town, so I decided to call you."

Ted knew why Mr. White had called him instead of Miss Monroe. If there was extra work to be done that evening, it would be up to Ted to do it. Of course it was still possible that Mr. Sawyer would show up. As a salesman he spent a good deal of time on the road. He may have been out of town himself, and was delayed getting back by bad roads. But Ted had not heard that he had failed to show up before, and coming right on the heels of Cliff's assertion of strange comings and goings at the Sawyer home, Ted found Mr. White's alarm rather contagious.

"All right, Mr. White, I'll come right down."

"Want me to drop over and pick you up?"

"No, I don't think so. I'll call Nelson. We may be able to use his help."

He depressed the cutoff button, released it, and dialed Nelson's number. Mrs. Morgan called Nelson to the phone.

"Say, Nel, can you pick me up and take me down to the *Town Crier* office? Things sound like they're in a jam down there."

"Okay, okay, Ted, don't press the panic button." This was a piece of slang they had picked up in college. It meant "keep your shirt on," but was a stronger term more suited to a nuclear age.

Realizing he had been speaking more loudly and excitedly than he intended, Ted lowered his voice. "Mr. Sawyer hasn't showed up, and we have to get the papers out."

"I know, I know. A paper isn't any good if you can't get it delivered. I'll be over in a few minutes."

He arrived on schedule, and they headed toward the office. On the way Ted told him what he knew of Mr. Sawyer's behavior. Nelson agreed it wasn't much to go on, but was a situation that ought to be watched.

"But our job is to get the paper out. Mr. Dobson can worry about the rest of it."

Ted thought that Mr. White looked relieved when they arrived.

"I'm sorry to admit that I know very little about this angle of the business," he told them. "I've never handled it before, and I've seldom been around while Mr. Oliver or Mr. Sawyer was working. I've always felt that when a man is doing his job you ought to let him alone to do it."

"I guess I don't know much about it either," Ted confessed. "I knew in a vague way that there was a lot of activity going on behind the scenes, but never bothered much about the details."

"How many different ways do you have of delivering papers?" asked Nelson. "I know in Forestdale you use boy carriers."

"Yes, and our only problem there is to deliver a bundle with the right number of papers to each carrier's home or pickup point. We have carriers beyond the edge of town, too—mostly farmers who are glad to pick up a little extra cash. The customers are too far apart for boys to walk, so we need older persons with cars. All these can wait till later, though. Our first problem is the bulldogs."

Nelson didn't know what bulldogs were, and having got them started counting out and bundling papers, Mr. White explained. "On a large city paper, the papers going out of town have to be dispatched earlier. This is called the bulldog edition. The city customers get a little later edition, which may have some later news items in it. The *Town Crier* isn't large enough to have facilities for adding news items during the middle of a run, so we have only one edition for each issue. Just the same, I've gotten into the habit of calling the out-of-town papers 'bulldogs.'"

"How are we going to handle the mailing?" Ted inquired.

The printer nodded toward a machine off to one side. "That's the addressing machine. Each paper has to be labeled and wrapped individually. Then we sort and bundle them by states, and deliver them to the post office. We would have to sort them by cities, too, except that we don't do enough mail business. There's no great rush about it, since the mail customers all get their paper a day late anyway. But it is a little bit tricky, so I think I'll do that part myself, after I'm sure I've got you boys started properly."

They were fortunate in that Mr. Sawyer had left his notebook, containing a careful and detailed record of where papers were to be delivered, how many, and by what time in case a train or bus schedule was involved.

"He's supposed to leave a record like that, just in case of mishap of some sort," Ted told Nelson, as they struggled with bailing wire to make each pile into a neat bundle, with extra papers wrapped around the side to keep them dry, and the carrier's name and number of papers placed on a tag attached to the top. "But you know how those records go. You never really expect someone else will have to take over, and sometimes it seems so much trouble to make little changes that you keep a lot of it up here." He tapped his head with his fingers.

"Not me," said Nelson with a laugh. "I don't file things in my head that I want to remember. They might get lost in the big empty spaces."

They worked hard for the next couple of hours, Ted and Nelson at the bundling, Mr. White at the addressing and mailing equipment. When he had finished his job, he came over to examine their work critically, but had to admit they had done a good enough job.

"Don't touch the mailing pieces, boys. I'll deliver them to the post office first thing in the morning. There's no sense in your waiting around for the post office to open. You think you could finish up the rest of this job without me? You're doing all right so far, and I really can't tell you anything more about how to do it, other than to follow Mr. Sawyer's list. And I don't want to be late getting down here tomorrow morning. I've got a full schedule of linotyping."

"I think we can handle it all right, Mr. White," Ted decided, and Nelson nodded his agreement.

"Sure we can. We've got a big chunk of it licked already, and the two of us together ought to be able to accomplish as much as Mr. Sawyer did by himself."

"That'll be fine, boys. Don't try to get down to the office tomorrow morning, Ted. I'll explain to Mr. Dobson what happened."

He left them, and they returned to their job. At one o'clock they had to stop, for the first of the trains leaving Forestdale was scheduled to depart at one thirty.

"Let's try to get *all* the papers for the trains in the car," Nelson suggested. "That way we'll only have to make one trip to the station."

"I guess that's what we're supposed to do," Ted agreed, after consulting Mr. Sawyer's schedule once more.

They began to carry bundles out to Nelson's car. The trunk was not large enough to hold all of them, and they piled other bundles into the back seat. It was a tight squeeze, but they made it. Leaving the light on behind them, Ted locked the office door, and they drove down to the station.

There was no trouble there, for the stationmaster knew exactly what to do with the papers. Nor did he seem especially surprised to see them. This was the holiday season, and many regular employees did take a little time off from work then. He showed them where to stack the papers, and promised to take care of the rest of it himself.

"We can help put them on the train," Nelson offered.

"Not unless you're magicians," he answered cheerfully. "It hasn't come in yet."

He assured them that there was no point in their waiting around, for Mr. Sawyer never did, gave them a receipt, and they left the nearly deserted station.

"I wonder how it pays to run trains with such a few passengers," Nelson remarked.

"Probably pick up commuters farther up the line. I wonder what did happen to Mr. Sawyer? If there'd been an accident, you'd think we would have heard by this time."

"Maybe he couldn't reach a phone. Or he may have tried and missed us. We weren't there all the time, and neither was Mr. White."

Back at the office, they were faced with more counting and bundling. Their next deadline was a bus leaving at four o'clock, and they hoped to have all the papers for the various busses ready for delivery by that time. They worked comfortably and easily, not feeling particularly rushed.

"You tired yet, Ted?"

"No. I was when we started, but I think I've got my second wind. Listen. Is that the phone?"

They had been making quite a bit of noise themselves, and the door to the office was closed, but as they quieted down they distinctly heard the ring. Ted ran toward the office. It was two o'clock, and a call coming at two o'clock in the morning was likely to be important. "Probably Mr. Sawyer," he called back.

He switched on the light and managed to reach the phone before it stopped ringing.

"*Town Crier* office."

"Oh, Mr. Dobson?"

Although he had never spoken to Mr. Sawyer over the telephone before, Ted felt certain that this really was their circulation manager. "No, this is Ted Wilford."

The man seemed not to have heard. "There's just one thing I want to say to you, Mr. Dobson, and that is I'm through with your crummy outfit for good. How do you like getting the papers out all by yourself? Not so easy as you tried to tell me, is it? It's worth overtime pay, isn't it? You aren't going to get a good man at straight time any more, but you're just silly enough to try."

Ted hardly knew what to say. It was Mr. Sawyer's voice, he thought, but the things he was saying didn't sound like Mr. Sawyer. Ted decided not to say anything more than necessary, but just to listen.

Mr. Sawyer continued, "I was just about ready to blow up when we had that argument last week, but I decided to wait till I had my pay check in my pocket, and then blow off. You're just tricky enough to try to hold up my pay, if you thought you could get away with it. No, you listen to me for once. This time I'm doing the talking. I had this all planned. I deliberately waited till Allison was out of town, so you'd have to do all this by yourself. Now I've got just one last thing to say, Mr. Dobson. I'm going to do you a favor. Go get my notebook and I'll tell you about a couple of changes."

Ted went to the back room, got the notebook, shook his head warningly as Nelson seemed about to ask a question, and returned to the phone.

"Okay," he said cautiously.

"See where it says 'Burton—Park Lane'? Well, don't deliver the papers to him—he's under quarantine and you might not get them back. They go to his substitute, John Maple, 315 Dell Drive. Got that? And that bus leaving for Silvertown at four o'clock. The schedule has been changed, and it now leaves at three o'clock. Got that? All right, then, I guess that's all. The only reason I bothered calling you is that I thought you might be calling *me* about it, and as far as I'm concerned I hope I never hear from your office again. What a sucker I've been, working for that kind of pay. Fortunately for me, I don't need that kind of money any more."

He banged the receiver in Ted's ear.

CHAPTER 7

THANKS FOR NOTHING

"That was Mr. Sawyer, wasn't it?" asked Nelson, who had heard only the few words Ted had to say.

"Yes, it was. He called up to quit, and almost blistered my ears off. And then he turned right around and tried to be helpful by calling my attention to a couple of changes on his list! Another thing was that he kept calling me Mr. Dobson."

"Maybe he didn't recognize your voice."

"No, maybe he didn't, but he would surely recognize Mr. Dobson's voice by now. Anyway, I told him I was Ted, but he didn't pay any attention."

"Why did he say he was quitting?"

"Oh, he said he'd had an argument with Mr. Dobson about money. He made it sound as though he'd just come into a pile of money and didn't need this job any more, so now he was glad of a chance to tell Mr. Dobson off."

"What do you think, Ted? Maybe he really did have some old grievances against Mr. Dobson. I know Mr. Dobson's got a reputation for being reasonable and generous, but his tongue can be kind of sharp at times, and he just might have gotten under Mr. Sawyer's skin sometime or other. Then if Mr. Sawyer had been brooding over it for a long time, built it up in his own mind—"

"I don't know. That doesn't sound like either Mr. Dobson or Mr. Sawyer. Anyway, I'll bet Mr. Sawyer knew all along that Mr. Dobson was out of town tonight. Mr. Dobson probably told him, just in case anything should come up."

Nelson thought this over for a few moments. "How do you figure it, Ted?"

"As it sounded to me, there must have been someone else listening to the conversation, someone at the other end that Mr. Sawyer wanted to impress."

"Maybe it was just his wife. Some men think they can make an impression on their wives by pretending to tell off the boss."

"I suppose that could be it, but somehow it sounds more important than that. I don't think Mr. Sawyer's a blow-off. He must have something serious on his mind. Look how this matches up with what Cliff told us. He said Mr. Sawyer's been acting kind of standoffish. And then there're those late visitors of his. He might have had a visitor there right now, and that was the person he was trying to impress. Of course I didn't want to give the show away, not until I know what kind of show it is."

"Well, what are we going to do about it?"

"What are we going to do? See that clock? If what Mr. Sawyer said about the change in the bus schedule is true, and I suppose it is, then we've got some stepping to do."

They returned to their job, and managed to finish the papers for the busses in time and deliver them to the depot. Their only remaining task at the office was to bundle the papers for the individual carriers.

"We've got some done already," Ted observed. "I suppose you could start delivering them while I finished up."

"No, we've still got time. I'm not sure about finding some of these places in the dark. If we're going to make any mistakes, let's make them together."

They were finished at the shop by four o'clock. "Now we take to the road," said Ted with relief.

"Where do we start—in town or out of town?"

Ted frowned. "The way it looks to me, we just follow the list right in order. That means out of town first."

"Well, that's reasonable," Nelson agreed. "I suppose it's more important to get the rural carriers started in plenty of time than it is those in town. Anyway, we won't be waking up as many people out in the country as we would here."

"You could get a new muffler and pay for it out of your check," Ted reminded him.

"What's wrong with my muffler?" Nelson demanded, stung. "It's a lot quieter than some I've heard." He looked thoughtful for a moment. "What's this about a check?"

"Why, sure, you knew Mr. Dobson would pay you for your work, didn't you?"

"Well, no, I didn't think about that. I thought I was just giving some assistance to a friend. I'll have to give that muffler idea some thought. You think I'm on a salary or what?"

"Hourly rate, plus mileage, is the usual way Mr. Dobson runs things."

Nelson brightened. "Well, that ought to give me enough to buy a new muffler, all right, if I decide I want one. This one *is* kind of quiet."

Their deliveries took them on a wide circuit of Forestdale, reaching as far out into the country as ten or fifteen miles. Driving conditions were not too good, but Nelson was a skilled and careful driver, and brought them through in good time and without mishap. Their circuit even took them into North Ridge, where they dropped off a large bundle. Although the larger town had its own paper, there were a good many people there who had connections of some kind in Forestdale, and so they read the *Town Crier* in addition to the *News-Record*. On the way home they stopped at an all-night place for hamburgers and hot malteds, which not only warmed them up but revived their spirits as well.

Returning to Forestdale, they were held up by a red light, for the signals were working in spite of the very light traffic. Nelson was forced to stop and wait, though it seemed there were no cars approaching from the cross street. Then, just as the signal light returned to caution, a car approached from their right. The signal had gone against it by the time it reached the intersection, but the driver went through just the same, and sped on his way. Nelson muttered an exclamation.

"That's just the way accidents happen. How'd he know but maybe I was idling back along this road, just ready to pick up speed as the light changed? We both go through at the same time, and bam! Maybe we'd both be dead, but I'd be *right.*"

But Ted was excited for a completely different reason. "Wasn't that Mr. Sawyer? It looked like him, and I think that's his make of car."

Nelson was less familiar with Mr. Sawyer's appearance than Ted, but he agreed about the car when he heard what make Mr. Sawyer drove. "It came from the direction of his home, too, and he must be headed out of town to the east. Wasn't there someone with him?"

"His wife was sitting beside him, and it looked like she was holding the baby. I suppose Tommy was stretched out on the back seat."

"What do you make of this, Ted?"

"It looks to me as though Mr. Sawyer made that call to me to impress a visitor, and that as soon as the visitor left they packed up and left town."

The taillights of Mr. Sawyer's car were just disappearing from view, for Nelson had remained stationary, and the light had changed against him again.

"Want to chase him, Ted?"

"No, what's the use? He'd only grow suspicious, with traffic as light as this. Besides, we've still got a job to do."

"Sure—*his* job. Well, I don't especially mind, but my mother sure is going to have a job if she tries to get me out of bed in the morning."

The greater part of the papers still remained to be delivered, for of course the *Town Crier* had its greatest circulation within the town itself. But they were on familiar ground here, and ran into no difficulties. They were finished before six thirty, which was the time the local boys were expected to start out on their routes. The *Town Crier* and breakfast went together on Tuesday and Friday in most Forestdale homes, for the big city daily to which most families subscribed did not arrive until late afternoon.

"And now to hit the hay," said Nelson with a big yawn.

"You really done in?"

"I wasn't, till I thought about bed. That did it." He drew up in front of Ted's home, and let him out. "See you in about a week, Ted."

"Oh, you'll see me before then—next Thursday night at the latest, if Mr. Sawyer doesn't come back, and it doesn't look as if he will."

In spite of his very late, or very early, bedtime, Ted was back at the office before noon. Mr. Dobson already knew some of the details of the night before from Mr. White, and Ted related the rest of the story to him.

"Very strange," said Mr. Dobson thoughtfully as Ted concluded. "That part about a quarrel—of course he never did have a quarrel with me. As a matter of fact he is getting a bonus for night work, and he's always expressed himself as well satisfied. I surely wouldn't blame a man if he decided he didn't want to work day and night, too, and I've always told Mr. Sawyer that he could leave any time he felt the long hours were getting him down. But he's always laughed off the idea."

"Do you think there's anything in what he said about not needing the money any more?"

"If he's come into any money, he's never mentioned it to me. But even supposing he did decide to leave, why not leave on a friendly basis? You never know when you may need a friend, and even if you were dissatisfied with the job, once you've decided to leave there's no longer any basis for argument. Are you sure you were talking to Mr. Sawyer, Ted?"

"Yes, I believe so, although his tone was very insolent. It sounded like his voice, and who else would have known about the changes in his schedule?"

"Yes, you must be right. I phoned his house this morning, and there was no answer. I also phoned long distance to the company where he works as a salesman. They didn't know just where he could be located, but that wasn't surprising, since he has quite a large territory which he covers on his own schedule. They were a little curious, but I didn't want to say anything that might jeopardize Mr. Sawyer's job with them, until I know a little better what's happening."

"Did Mr. Sawyer know you were out of town last night, Mr. Dobson?"

"Oh, yes. I told him when he came in last Saturday for his pay check."

"Then he knew when he called that he wasn't going to find you here, but he carried the bluff just the same."

"Yes, Ted. Mr. Sawyer seems a very conscientious man, and I imagine his real reason for calling was to make sure the paper *was* getting out on schedule and that you weren't running into any difficulties. Of course he didn't express it in those terms. I'm not at all sure another person was listening at his end. He may have spoken to you that way simply because he has some private business of his own that he wanted to be sure you stay out of."

"Then why did he call me Mr. Dobson?"

"That's true. It certainly suggests that he was trying to convey some message to you that he wasn't able to express directly."

"Whatever it was, it didn't get through to me."

The arrival of Andy put an end to the conversation, as Ted sensed Mr. Dobson did not care to discuss the matter in front of an outsider. Then Ted decided to go out to lunch. It seemed silly to leave so soon after he had arrived, but he had not stopped for breakfast at home that morning, wanting to catch Mr. Dobson before noon. He returned to the office in time to watch the finish of Andy's demonstration, and to help him put his equipment away.

"I suppose you'll be leaving us next week," Ted observed.

"Yes, but I'll have my busiest time just before that, grading the contest entries when they come in. I'll have to punch up a card for each entry, and then I'm hoping Lulu will be able to select the winners, right out here in plain view of whoever cares to watch. It'll be a little tricky, since I'll have to guard against any errors I might make myself, but I think I can work it out."

"That ought to be interesting. Lulu really is quite a girl."

"That's no lie," said Andy, almost with affection. "Most remarkable of all, no one really understands her capacity. Already we've found that Lulu can do things that the persons who designed her never dreamed of. Lulu can give the right answers, but it's up to the person operating her to give the right questions."

"I don't think I quite understand that," Ted objected.

"Well, suppose you gave Lulu a difficult mathematical equation to solve. Lulu would give you the answer. But the answer Lulu gave would have no significance to you, unless the equation you gave to her was somehow significant to you. That's the problem, to ask the right questions; that is, to pose the sort of problem that Lulu can solve by calculation. It's a scientific maxim that knowing the right questions to ask is the first step in finding the right answers."

"Do you have other demonstrations like this lined up, after you leave here?" Ted wanted to know.

"Well, not quite like this. We're not really interested in the contest angle, of course. I work as a good-will man for the company making these machines. They're interested in showing these machines off to the public, demonstrating the different things they can do, gaining public acceptance of them, and possibly steering young people into careers with these machines. There's no immediate profit to the company, but there may be a long-range benefit."

As Andy was putting some of his folders up onto a shelf, his sleeve fell back, and Ted noticed a tattoo upon his wrist, with the initials A. M.

"Were you in the navy, Andy?"

"Yes, I put in my hitch. It's been a family tradition. My father wanted me to join."

Then he turned abruptly away, as though he had made a mistake in mentioning his family, and Ted was forced to drop the subject. Andy left a few minutes later.

This was a fairly leisurely time for Ted. His next deadline was Thursday noon, still two days away, although of course it wouldn't do to leave too many things until the last minute. Whether he covered his usual beat that afternoon was of little consequence, since he could pick up everything the next day, if necessary. But just in case something might have come up which would require a follow-up, he decided to go that day. He was disappointed to find that Sergeant Jeffers had nothing much for him.

"Just a few more petty thefts, Ted, and I don't think you want those."

However, it was the best he had, and just for the sake of having a complete record of them in case anything should come up, Ted dutifully wrote down the items. Kirtland's had been victimized again, as well as several smaller stores. Once again the items were small in value.

"He'll never get rich at this rate," Ted remarked.

"Not by the time he pays his income tax on this stuff," the sergeant agreed with a laugh.

Although Ted did not care to admit it, he was disappointed about one particular thing. He had thought that possibly Mr. Sawyer's strange actions had somehow involved him with the police, and that there might be some indication of it on the police blotter. However, there was nothing to help Ted on this matter.

He returned to the office, where he set about helping Miss Monroe with the mail as he had done the previous day. Several more thank-you notes had come in and Ted was assigned to copying these.

The first two gave him no trouble, but the third letter caused him to blink.

"What do you make of this, Miss Monroe?" he asked, passing the letter over to her.

She read it carefully, without discovering what he meant. "What's wrong with it?"

"Do you recognize the name?"

"Yes, Mrs. Klein. She's a widow with several children. I remember her very well from our list."

"I know, but do you know when we printed that item?"

Then she caught on, and was as perplexed as he was. "Why, we just printed that letter in this morning's paper!"

"Yes, and she wrote a letter *yesterday* thanking us for what we did for her. Want me to show it to Mr. Dobson?"

"Yes, you'd better, Ted. This could lead to complications."

The editor had been busy on the phone, and so had not heard this conversation. Ted took the letter to his desk, and called his attention to the discrepancy. His employer looked worried.

"I don't like to have us take credit for doing something we didn't do, Ted, but that's not the most important thing. We do our best to safeguard these names, and if they've somehow leaked out, I don't like it a bit."

"Isn't it possible that she has other friends who know of her troubles, and decided to help her out directly?"

"That's possible, of course, Ted. But the fact that she thanked *us* would seem to indicate that she doesn't know of any such people, and believes we did it all. I believe I'll call her and tell her we didn't send the things, and incidentally find out exactly what she did receive. I know that our article asked for toys for the three children."

There was a short delay in reaching Mrs. Klein, since she did not have a phone herself, but depended upon the phone of her downstairs neighbor. However, she came on shortly, and apparently thanked Mr. Dobson once again.

"I'm sorry, Mrs. Klein, but we had nothing to do with these gifts. Our item was only printed this morning. They must have come from other friends of yours... Would you mind telling me what gifts you received?... I see. Well, thank you very much, Mrs. Klein. I'm sure it must be all right, and merry Christmas to you!"

Mr. Dobson hung up and turned to the others. "She said she doesn't know of anyone else who could have sent the things, though she'd like to thank them. The toys she received were one for each of her three children: a doll stroller for the little girl, a tricycle for the little boy, and a Chinese puzzle game for the older boy."

Something clicked in Ted's memory. "A doll stroller, a tricycle, and a Chinese puzzle? Why, those were the three things stolen from Kirtland's last week!"

CHAPTER 8

OUT TO LEE'S END

Mr. Dobson, Miss Monroe, and Ted were gathered in a tense little group. It was true that the items stolen had no great value, but still the implications could be very serious.

"I suppose stealing things to give them away to needy people is a crime," said Ted slowly, "but somehow it doesn't seem so bad as a lot of other crimes. I always liked the Robin Hood stories, and that was one of the things he did."

The editor shook his head. "We now have legitimate ways of helping needy people. When an individual decides to take all this responsibility on himself, it suggests that he is badly out of touch with his environment. Furthermore, it makes you want to find out how out of touch he really is. Such a person could be headed for serious trouble."

Miss Monroe had a suggestion. "I think we ought to get all these thank-you notes together, and read them over again. Now that I think of it, several of the letters read rather strangely. I wonder if anyone else has been thanking us for things we never sent them."

She procured the letters from the files, and read them over again, checking them against the case histories as they had been printed in the newspaper. Many of the letters were expressed in such general terms that it was impossible to tell. But at least two letters mentioned "gifts," whereas the *Town Crier* had sent only one gift. And one letter definitely did thank them for a baby's play pen which they had never sent. Miss Monroe had wondered about it at the time, but passed it off as a mistake. A play pen had appeared on the police list that very day, Ted recalled, although it may have been missing for quite a few days before the loss was discovered and reported to the police.

"I believe I'll call these two parties on their 'gifts,'" Mr. Dobson decided. "That ought to help us decide whether we're on the right track or not."

He put through the calls, and the results were the same. Two more items, like those reported to the police, had been given out as gifts. Such a series of happenings could hardly be mere coincidence.

"What we could do is call everybody," Ted suggested. "Then we'd know all the items that were received, and we'd have a complete check."

"No, Ted, I don't think that will be necessary. It would only start a good many people wondering what was going on, and I think we've already proved our point. Somebody has definitely been stealing things—usually toys or other items for children—and giving them as gifts. I wonder how the time element checks out? I asked these people I called if they had received their gifts before their items were printed in the paper, but they weren't sure about it. We do know that it happened that way at least once, but that doesn't necessarily mean the thief knew about our list ahead of time. He may just have known about Mrs. Klein's case through some other means."

"But he did know about the three children," Miss Monroe put in. "He had an appropriate gift for each one. Our article gave the ages. And if he had known Mrs. Klein personally, he still wouldn't have known that toys were the things specifically requested."

"No, possibly not, though it would be a natural thing to think of a toy apiece for each of the children."

Ted had been waiting for a chance to mention a new discovery which had just occurred to him. "Miss Monroe, do you have a list of all the stores taking part in our contest? Today's paper only printed the names of the remaining stores. Thank you. Now here's something. I've got a list of stores reporting missing items to the police. Except for Kirtland's, every store that has something stolen is entered in our contest."

The others were surprised by this sudden revelation. Ted had another hunch, and drew up a chair. He took out his pencil and did some quick checking, while Mr. Dobson and Miss Monroe looked over his shoulder. His calculations verified his hunch.

"Look again how the time checks out. We can't tell exactly when the items were stolen from the stores, because the loss might not have been reported promptly. But every loss occurred sometime after that store had its day for our contest. In no case was a loss reported *before* the contest day. And look, counting today, there are still five stores waiting to participate in the contest, and not one of these has reported a theft as yet."

Mr. Dobson looked very much disturbed. "Still, not *all* the stores in the contest have reported losses," he pointed out.

"No, but we can't be sure all the losses have been reported anyway. Sometimes the store might not have missed the article, or thought it was mislaid or broken, or if the amount wasn't very great they decided not to report it. After all, they're all pretty busy just before Christmas."

"I think Ted's hit it," Miss Monroe decided shrewdly. "We may not have a complete list of all items stolen, and we probably don't have a complete list of all the extra gifts given out to persons mentioned in our columns. But I have a suspicion that if we did have complete lists, we'd find that the items were exactly the same. I'd be willing to bet that every store in our contest has been victimized."

"And the gifts have been made to persons *before* they were mentioned in our paper, at least in some cases," Ted added.

The editor shook his head slowly and sorrowfully. "Even though we can't prove it conclusively, there's strong evidence to believe that you are both right. It would appear that everywhere Santa Claus goes, something is stolen. He has access to Kirtland's, of course, and he's called on each of the stores in our contest so far. I'm afraid Mr. Gentry has been taking his Santa Claus job too seriously. He's beginning to get the idea he really is Santa Claus."

"That big sack of his must be very useful to him," Ted observed. "He could carry almost anything away in that. It would even hold a tricycle, if it were placed there properly. And things like a doll stroller and a baby's play pen might not be too hard to handle, for they fold up. I suppose it wouldn't be much of a problem for Santa Claus to steal toys, since he's right around that department anyway, and probably shows off toys to the children sometimes."

"Would Mr. Gentry have any way of knowing the names and addresses of these people in our column?" asked Miss Monroe.

"I think he would if he really cared to," said the editor thoughtfully. "He's come in almost every day, you know, and I think there have been occasions when he was alone in the office. I remember that at least once or twice I was called back to the printing room while he was here, and I left him sitting here alone for a few minutes. I suppose he could have done some snooping then."

"I don't suppose it would do any good to go to the police about this," Miss Monroe offered. "I hardly think any of the stores would care to prosecute, in view of the small amounts, and the fact that he wasn't trying to profit himself but only to help other people. Mr. Kirtland would have been glad to donate the things, if he'd been asked."

"No, I don't think it's a police matter just yet," said Mr. Dobson cautiously. "We have our suspicions, but very little that would stand up in court. Anyway, I wouldn't care to involve the police unless I felt sure that was the best way of handling things. Mr. Gentry certainly isn't the ordinary type of criminal. It may be that he's just a confused old man in special need of help."

"Do you think we ought to notify Mr. Kirtland?" asked Ted. "I suppose if we did he'd fire him."

"No, Ted, I don't think I'd care to do that just now, either. There is still a matter of proof, but I have an idea that we'll have that proof very soon, now that we know what to look for. Which store has the contest display today—Shilling's Dry-Goods Store, isn't it? Now let's figure it out—what would he be likely to take from a dry-goods store? Have any of our cases asked for items likely to be found there, Miss Monroe?"

"There's Mrs. Vance's case, coming up in our last column, for next Friday's paper. She's asking for clothing for her children."

"Then I think we've hit it. There seems a very good chance that Mr. Gentry will take something from the dry-goods store today that would help fill that request. Chances are he'll send it right on to Mrs. Vance, and that she'll receive it either tomorrow or Thursday—before the item has even appeared in print. That ought to give us all the proof we'll need—if it happens."

And it was very likely to happen, Ted thought. Once you have caught on to a thief's pattern of operation, it is often possible to anticipate what he will do next, and this generally leads to his undoing.

"But how did Mr. Gentry expect to get away with this? He was certain to get caught sooner or later, wasn't he?"

"Maybe not, Ted. Some of the stores would report thefts to the police, but with all the milling holiday crowds that wouldn't prove a very strong link with Santa Claus. And the fact that these things were later sent to needy people wouldn't have been very strong proof against Santa Claus. It might never have been noticed that the items were the same. The only way we caught on was that Mrs. Klein happened to send a thank-you note before we'd sent her anything, and this started you wondering. Mr. Gentry couldn't have anticipated anything like that."

"Then we let everything go until tomorrow?"

"No, I don't want to 'let it go' exactly, Ted. I don't like to delay on important matters. I think it's important to prevent any more of these thefts, although unfortunately we're too late to do anything about Shilling's store today. But I do think we can do a little quiet checking up. Will you get Mr. Gentry's personnel card from the file, Miss Monroe?"

She brought the card, then returned to her desk as the editor studied it, with Ted close by.

"You know, Ted, that everyone working for the paper, even part time, has to fill out one of these cards. We need addresses, social-security numbers, number of dependents, and things like that. That reminds me, you'll have to ask Nelson to fill out one of these cards, too."

"Then he's working for the paper?"

"It would certainly seem so, Ted." Mr. Dobson smiled. "He put in a good night's work last night, and we'll be calling on him again. I don't think I've thanked you boys for the way you filled in during the emergency, but I appreciate it very much. It was fortunate that it happened during the holidays, when the two of you were available."

"I wonder," said Ted moodily.

"Wonder what, Ted?"

"Why it happened during the holidays. Maybe Mr. Sawyer *knew* there'd be someone available to fill in, and that's why he did it just then."

"It's a possibility, though the rest of the things he did don't seem to make any kind of sense."

"Are you going to do anything about replacing Mr. Sawyer?"

"Not just yet, Ted. As long as I've got you and Nelson to depend on, I think I'll let it go for a while. Something may develop yet. And I don't think Mr. Sawyer would dare stay out of touch very long with the company for which he works. It may be that I'll get a lead from them in a few days about where he can be found."

The editor studied Mr. Gentry's card.

"There doesn't seem to be a great deal here that is helpful. He was formerly an electrical engineer, and as such he traveled about a great deal. It would appear that he had neither a fixed home nor a family of any kind. He's living at present all alone in a big house on Walpole Avenue. A single person would hardly need such a big house, but I believe he mentioned that the family is spending the winter in Florida, so he was able to rent it cheap. It seems that he gave up engineering about a year ago, and that he was unemployed for quite a few months before coming to Kirtland's. Where it asks, 'Reason for leaving previous employment,' he answers, 'Effects of an auto accident.' Hmm, that might be interesting. I'd like to know more about that accident. It must have had a serious effect on him to cause him to leave his job."

"Is there any way of finding out?"

"There may be. I believe I'll call Mr. Kirtland on his private line and ask him confidentially where the accident occurred. If it isn't too far away, perhaps you could look into it."

He put through the call, and after a short delay was given the information he wanted. He hung up and explained to Ted, "It was at Lee's End. That's only about thirty miles from here. Do you want to go?"

"In your car?"

"Well, it would be a little handier for me if Nelson would drive you—if he doesn't mind working during vacation."

"Oh, no, I'm sure he doesn't mind, if you don't mind listening to him gripe about how much he hates work."

Mr. Dobson smiled. "I'm sure I can stand it if he can."

Ted called Nelson. "Come on down, boy, you're working for the paper." His friend groaned, but was down at the office within a few minutes. He had to fill out his personnel card, which he did while Ted explained what they were up to, and then they were ready to leave.

"Is there anything in particular you want me to find out, Mr. Dobson?"

"No—just things such as: was he hurt, who was responsible, what were the damages, was there any sort of settlement or legal action. I can only guess what happened from this distance, so you'll have to use your own judgment."

The roads had been cleared, but there was still a remnant of slushy snow which made driving slow.

"If it wasn't for that, we could make it in jig time," Ted remarked.

"I thought you liked snow."

"I do, but it's something you can get tired of awfully fast."

"Lee's End is a funny name. Do you happen to know why they call it that? It sounds like the end of a point of land."

"I think it means the end of the railroad," Ted recollected. "They named it in the days when a town's whole life depended upon the railroad. They had a little spur off the main line that went up to Lee's End and stopped there."

"Well, they must have a road now, if that's where the accident happened," Nelson replied.

An hour later they were approaching Lee's End.

"I suppose the police station, fire station, town hall, and everything are all in the same building," Nelson mused. "Who are you going to talk to, the police chief? If you get to a sergeant he'll probably be the head of the whole department."

"Maybe not. See that marker?" It gave the name Lee's End, followed by the abbreviation *Twp.*

"What's that stand for—twirp?"

"It means *township,* and that means it's probably spread over a lot larger territory than a town. It may be bigger than it looks. Well, let's find the town hall, or whatever they have."

CHAPTER 9

A BUMP ON THE HEAD

As Nelson had predicted, they soon found themselves in conversation with a sergeant—Sergeant Walker.

Walker puckered his brows for a few moments, as though recollecting. "Yes, I remember that accident. They were the first traffic fatalities we'd had in three years. But with the new stateway coming through here, I suppose we'll be getting our share."

"Then there was someone killed?" Ted questioned.

"Two people—Mr. and Mrs. Malcolm."

"They were in the other car?"

"There wasn't any other car. They were passengers with Mr. Gentry. He must have skidded off the road, or fallen asleep, or something like that. He was pretty vague on how it happened. That's not surprising, though. After a person gets a severe bump on the head, he will often be unable to remember what happened to him several hours before the accident. I suppose there's some sort of explanation for that, but I don't know what it is."

"Then Mr. Gentry was badly injured, too?"

"Well, considering what happened to his passengers, he got out of it pretty fortunately. He was able to crawl out of the car and go for help. But he didn't escape altogether. Besides the bump on the head, there were other scratches and bruises, and some internal injuries. It kept him in a hospital bed for more than two weeks, and I don't think he was completely recovered when he was discharged."

"He wasn't arrested?"

"No, it's pretty hard to prove negligence in a case like that, and nobody pushed it. Maybe there wasn't anybody left to do it. I don't know."

"Did Mr. Gentry or Mr. and Mrs. Malcolm live in Lee's End, or were they just passing through?"

"Just passing through. I'd never met any of them before. If you want to know where they lived, wait a minute and I'll check the police report."

He left them, and presently returned with a large file. He thumbed through it, moistening his finger from time to time, and soon found the case.

"Mr. and Mrs. Malcolm lived in Sou'western. If you want to find out anything more about them, I suppose you could inquire there. Mr. Gentry was a traveling engineer, and apparently didn't have any permanent address, except his company."

"But I understand he never went back to work with the company. Was that due to his injuries, do you suppose, or was he near retiring age anyway?"

"No, I don't think he was old enough to retire. I imagine he'd still be with the company, if it hadn't been for the accident. Of course I never doubted that he was injured physically, but the doctors seemed to think he'd get over that all right. No, I've always had a hunch it was the bump on the head that affected him. I'd never talked to him before the accident so I don't know how he was then, but after the accident he struck me as kind of strange—not the sort of person you'd imagine being a successful engineer. His job just didn't seem important to him any more. I don't think he wanted to go back."

Since this seemed to be about all that Walker could tell them, they thanked him and left. Out on the road Nelson asked:

"Well, is that it, or do we go on from here?"

"What did Sergeant Walker mean when he said Sou'western? I suppose he meant Southwestern, but southwestern what? I was going to ask, but you looked like you knew, so I didn't."

"Sou'western—that's really the name, with an apostrophe and all. It's a little town about forty miles the other side of Forestdale. I've noticed it on large-scale road maps."

"You mean it's seventy miles from where we are now? Then I guess that ends it for today. We'll report back to Mr. Dobson and see what he says about it. This may give him everything he needs, and maybe that bump on the head accounts for everything. According to Walker, it seemed to change Mr. Gentry's personality."

"The only trouble with that idea, Ted, is that everybody's had a conk on the noggin at some time or other. If you want to know why the whole world's crazy, you could stop right there."

"Well, I didn't mean it in exactly that way. I meant that if he felt responsible for the accident—and it looks like it must have been his fault—it's no wonder that he became melancholy."

They drove on in silence for a few miles. At length Nelson said:

"This is all interesting enough, Ted, about a Santa Claus being a thief and giveaway artist all at once, and I can see why Mr. Dobson should be concerned about clearing it up, as long as the newspaper's involved in it. But what's it add up to, after all? Meanwhile, I think we're losing sight of something else that's a good deal more important. That's Mr. Sawyer. What's he been up to, and where is he now? We ought to be doing something about that."

"What is there we can do? You got any ideas?"

"No, but it's just possible that Cliff Corby has. He knew more about Mr. Sawyer than we did—I mean about his home life, and I've got a notion that's where the mystery's centered. I think the three of us ought to go into a huddle about it tonight and see if we can figure out anything."

"At your house or mine?"

"Cliff's will be better. We'll be right on the scene there, and that may help us. Heck, maybe Mr. Sawyer's back home already for all we know. I'll call Cliff, and if he can make it I'll pick you up, say about nine, and take you over."

It was dark by the time they reached Forestdale. The *Town Crier* office was closed, and Ted said he would call Mr. Dobson at home that evening to tell him the results of their trip.

"Ask him if he wants me to report for work tomorrow," Nelson requested, "and if so, what time."

Ted made the call after supper, and explained to the editor everything they had discovered. When Ted was finished Mr. Dobson said:

"I'd say you've done a good job, Ted. That accident could explain a number of things."

"Do you think we ought to go on to Sou'western and inquire from there?"

"I suppose you should, Ted, eventually, but I don't think there's any rush about it. The most important thing right now is to make sure these robberies aren't repeated. The next is to try to establish proof of Mr. Gentry's guilt, and the last is to decide what action to take. I don't like to look on this as a police matter. At the same time it would be irresponsible and possibly dangerous to ignore it, for we can't be sure what he might do next. I think Mr. Gentry is a badly troubled man, and that it is up to his friends to try to help him. I'm sure something can be worked out after Christmas that will be satisfactory to all persons concerned. That's when it may be useful to try to locate old friends who knew him before the accident. What they have to say about his character and background may help us reach a decision on what action to take."

"By the way, Nelson wanted to know if he should report tomorrow."

"Yes, ask him to report in the afternoon if he can, will you? I'm sure we'll have a great many more donations to pick up and deliver."

"Will you want me to go with him?"

"No, I'm afraid the work at the office will be piling up, and besides I have something else in mind for you. I'll tell you tomorrow."

Nelson picked up Ted at nine, and they went over to Cliff's. He took them upstairs to his room, overlooking his back yard, with Mr. Sawyer's yard beyond.

"Let's keep the light off," Nelson suggested, "and see whether we can catch anything going on at Mr. Sawyer's."

"Have you noticed anything there yet, Cliff?" asked Ted.

"Not a thing," Cliff returned, for Nelson had already told him about the events of the previous evening. "There's been no sign of life there all day that I've seen—and I've been interested enough to keep looking over there every little while all day long, even before Nel told me what happened. My mother's been pretty curious about things, too."

"Why?" asked Nelson. "She doesn't know anything about last night, does she?"

"No, but she's had her eye on Mr. Sawyer's place for a while. She's kind of taken a fancy to little Tommy, and he used to come over for cookies once in a while. But she says she hasn't seen him out playing for over a week."

"Why didn't your mother go over and ask if she really wanted to know?" Ted questioned.

"Well, she doesn't know Mrs. Sawyer very well, and she didn't want to seem nosy, especially after what Dad said about Mr. Sawyer's being so cool. Anyway, she thought maybe Mrs. Sawyer was a little bit peeved over Tommy's asking for cookies all the time, and was keeping him home."

"Is that all we're going to do," Nelson complained, "just sit here in the dark and watch? We can put on the radio, can't we?"

"Sure." Cliff switched it on to a dance-music program. "You might even dance, if you can find a partner. That radio's a good idea, though, for my dad might think we were planning on robbing a bank. Then he'd be mad because we left him out."

"If we came over here to figure out what's happened to Mr. Sawyer, I think we ought to get started," Ted interposed. "Let's pool all our knowledge and see if it adds up to anything."

"All right, Ted, you start," Cliff encouraged him.

"Well, Mr. Sawyer's been working for the *Town Crier* for a number of months, and there's never been any trouble with him before. You've known him as a neighbor, and he's made a good impression on you, too. I think that eliminates any likelihood that Mr. Sawyer is involved in anything shady or crooked. But I don't believe there's any doubt that he's in some kind of terrible trouble. Whatever this trouble is, it's something he doesn't want his friends to know about, and he doesn't want their help."

"How about money troubles?" suggested Nelson.

"I don't know about that. Of course I do know that he's not rich or anything like that, and he's always been glad to earn extra money when he could. But it seems to me if he had money troubles, he wouldn't try to solve them by acting the way he's been acting. He'd be *more* interested in working. And if he really was badly in need of a loan, and couldn't get it anywhere else, I think he'd feel that he could go to Mr. Dobson with his problem. Then, too, the way he talked to me on the phone didn't lead me to feel he was very much interested in money right now. I don't think that's his difficulty."

"What about the way he left town early this morning?" Nelson pointed out. "I know some people prefer to drive during the night when traffic's lighter—but not in this bad weather, and not when you have little children to take along."

"Then what do you think he was doing?" asked Cliff.

"I think he was *running away* from something, something he was afraid of."

"If he was afraid, why didn't he go to the police?"

"That's easy enough to say, but sometimes something might come up where'd you feel that the police are not competent enough to safeguard you. And a man wouldn't want to take risks with his family. I'll bet that's it," said Nelson, growing excited. "I'll bet he sneaked out of town the way he did because he wants to take his family some place where he thinks they'll be safe."

"Then why are we watching his house? I thought this was *your* idea. If he's hiding out somewhere, he won't be back."

"Wait a minute, we can't be sure about that," Ted came in. "How far can a man run, after all? He's quit his job at the *Town Crier.* If he quits his salesman's job, too, then what's his family going to do? And wherever he goes, he still can't be sure his problem won't catch up with him. It seems to me he might be worried about his family, but after he's made sure they're as safe as possible, he might come back to make a deal, or somehow try to get rid of his problem."

"Have you anything to add to this, Cliff?" asked Nelson.

"No, except to agree pretty much with everything you've said. As I mentioned before, we don't know the Sawyers very well, but isn't there some way we could find out more about them?"

Nelson pounded his fist into his hand. "How about the personnel cards at the *Town Crier* office, Ted? They ask a lot of questions. Mr. Sawyer must have filled out one of those. There's one question that asks for the name of your closest relative outside your immediate family. I suppose they ask that so if you move they'll have someone else they can inquire about you. Couldn't we tell from the card if Mr. Sawyer has any relatives around here? And there might be other things besides."

"I suppose there might," Ted agreed slowly. "But I don't like to sneak a look at those cards without asking Mr. Dobson's permission. I suppose the name of a relative *might* be very important, if that happened to be the place the family's hiding out, but I don't like to tell Mr. Dobson a lot of our suspicions until we have something to back them up."

"Even if Mr. Sawyer does come back to the house," Cliff observed, "there's no particular reason it's got to be tonight. But I suppose we ought to watch just the same. How're we going to set it up? You fellows want to stay here all night?"

"Well, I don't know," Ted objected. "I was up all last night, and I don't think I could stay awake another night."

"You don't have to. You can lie down on the bed. What about you, Nel?"

"Oh, I don't feel very tired, and I don't have to get up as early as Ted. But if I'm going to stay I'll have to call home."

"Me, too," Ted added.

"All right, then, come on."

Nelson and Ted made their calls, and the three friends returned to Cliffs room. Ted sat down where he could keep his eye on the house to the rear, while Cliff maneuvered the knobs on his radio. He finally got something that sounded very distant and foreign, and settled back until he could learn its point of origin. Then his mind returned to the problem facing them.

"I guess we're all agreed that Mr. Sawyer is in some sort of trouble, but we still don't know what sort of trouble it is." His voice trailed off, and they waited for him to continue. "Oh, oh."

"What's the matter?" asked Nelson.

"I'm not sure," said Cliff, his tone suddenly very quiet and sober. "The most terrible thought just came to me."

"Well, what is it?" Nelson demanded impatiently.

"I hate even to say it. You guys will think I'm way off base, but do you think there's any chance Tommy's been kidnapped?"

CHAPTER 10

THE VIGIL

The light from the radio pilot light was sufficient to show the others' startled faces.

"Kidnapped!" exclaimed Ted.

"How could it be—I mean, why?" Nelson objected. "Their family isn't rich."

"How do you know? They might not be rich themselves, but they might have a rich relative on whom they can call. Or there might be some other reason for a kidnapping besides ransom money."

"Like what?"

"Maybe somebody's trying to bring pressure on Mr. Sawyer to get him to do something he doesn't want to do. Threatening his family might be the best way to do it."

"What do you think?" asked Nelson, turning to Ted for his opinion.

"Well, I suppose there's at least a hundred-to-one chance against it," said Ted slowly. "The trouble is that once one of these terrible possibilities occurs to you, it's hard to be reasonable about it again. What made you think of kidnapping, Cliff?"

"I don't know exactly, but suddenly everything seemed to fit together better that way. My mother hasn't seen Tommy for a week. Then you didn't see him in the car when the family left town. You thought he was sleeping in the back seat, but you can't be sure about that. Then we agreed that Mr. Sawyer was in some sort of jam that he didn't want his friends to know about. That made it look like a kidnapping, too. Usually people try to avoid publicity until they see if they can get the victim back safely. Another thing is the way the family ran away as though it wanted to hide. That indicates danger of some sort. Mr. Sawyer may have been trying to protect the *rest* of his family. And he quit his job at the *Town Crier* suddenly, too."

"Why did he do that?" asked Ted. "Usually kidnapers want you to go along with your regular business, so no one gets suspicious."

"Yes, but not a *newspaper.* If they know about Mr. Dobson, they'd want to be sure that Mr. Sawyer stayed as far away from him as possible."

"Holy smokes!" exclaimed Nelson. "If we're mixed up in a kidnapping, this is the deepest water we've ever been in. We'd better tread water pretty carefully."

"Yes, I agree that we'd better be awfully careful," Ted advised, "no matter what the trouble is. I suppose it *could* be a kidnapping, but a couple of things argue against it. One is that I've been around the police station the last couple of days, and I didn't pick up any rumor about it. Of course if the police were covering up while the parents attempted to make a deal with the kidnapers, there wouldn't be any official record of it yet. But still you'd think there'd be an air of undercover activity or excitement around the station. I didn't notice anything like that. Things seemed fairly dull down there. In a case like this, very often the police will tip off the newspaper, and ask it to keep it quiet. They do this because they know a reporter is nosing around anyway, and they're afraid he might uncover something that will give the show away."

"Maybe the police don't know about it," Nelson pointed out. "Everybody who's had any experience with it says that the best thing to do in a case like this is to notify the police, but not all parents would agree with that. All they're interested in is getting the child back. Afterward the police can worry about catching the criminals."

"Another thing," Ted went on, "is the time element. Mr. Sawyer became cool, and Mrs. Sawyer stopped Tommy from coming over more than a week ago. It's hard to cover up a kidnapping for that long a time. The school may inquire why he's absent—"

"Tommy's only four," Cliff interposed. "He doesn't go to school."

"Anyway, friends or relatives may drop over. You just can't keep a child out of sight for very long before somebody misses him. You can make up a story that will satisfy casual acquaintances or neighbors, but it is pretty hard to fool anyone very intimate with you. Besides, how many mothers wouldn't go into hysterics if this happened to them?"

"He may not have been kidnapped a week ago. Maybe the family just received threats, and they're hiding out as a precaution."

"I don't think kidnapers are likely to send threats that would put a family on its guard—not if they really mean business. However, I agree that it *might* be a kidnapping, or something else nearly as bad."

"If it is a kidnapping," asked Nelson, "what do we do about it—notify the police?"

Ted shook his head vigorously. "Not the police, or Mr. Dobson, or even our own parents. We might think Mr. and Mrs. Sawyer were doing the wrong thing, but nevertheless the decision is theirs to make, and I wouldn't want to do anything to interfere with it. We'll just keep our noses out of it, unless it appears that there's some way we can help them."

"If we keep our noses out of it, how will we know if we can help them or not?" Nelson demanded.

"Well, I don't think it will hurt if we stay on the fringes and be careful. Watching their house isn't going to hurt anybody, and might give us a clue that will help. And I'll find some way of looking at Mr. Sawyer's personnel card at the office. I don't like to sneak behind Mr. Dobson's back, but he's concerned about Mr. Sawyer, and as long as there's a chance this is a kidnapping, we have to keep it as quiet as possible." He went on, after a moment's thought, "I think there's just one thing that gives me the right to interfere. When Mr. Sawyer called, it seemed to me he was trying to convey a message of some sort. It's as though he were saying, 'Don't pay any attention to my words. What I'm really trying to say is something I don't dare put into words.' I wonder what it was?"

No one had an answer so Ted relinquished his observation post to Nelson, while he stretched out on the bed. In spite of the worry in the back of their minds, Cliff continued to fiddle with the short-wave set, and from time to time was able to interest them in a reception from some distant point.

Ted dozed until he was awakened by a hand shaking his shoulder roughly, while another hand was laid warningly across his lips. The radio was still on, and someone was talking in a foreign language.

"All right, I'm awake," he whispered, sitting up. "What's happening?"

"A car pulled into the Sawyer driveway—and it's not Mr. Sawyer's," Cliff said.

"What time is it?"

"Two-thirty."

"What about the driver?"

"He went into the Sawyer house."

"Where? I don't see a light on."

"No, but he's in there all right. He may be in the front of the house."

"What do you think we'd better do—waylay the driver?" asked Nelson.

"No, I don't see how we can," said Ted reflectively. "We don't dare give anything away till we know what the score is. I'd like to get the license number of that car, though. It might be useful later."

"Then let's get it!" suggested Cliff. "I think we can do it. The car is almost in front of the Sawyer garage. We can sneak back alongside both garages, and get the license without exposing ourselves."

"I guess it's worth a try, if you really think we can do it."

Cliff led the way downstairs in the dark. In the kitchen he opened and closed the refrigerator ("Just to let my mother think we came down for something to eat," he explained), and then very quietly opened the back door.

"This way," he whispered, and the others followed closely behind.

Silently they crept along the narrow passage between the Corby garage and the fence. There was another passage of a similar nature in the Sawyer yard. Fortunately this particular part of the two yards had been sheltered from the snow, which was lying in high drifts in many other places. As they reached the Sawyer yard, Cliff whispered back:

"Better let me go on alone. I know the obstacles better, and we don't want to make any noise."

Accordingly Ted and Nelson hung back while Cliff crept quietly forward. It occurred to Ted they were facing the danger that the man might have come out by this time, and be sitting in his car. However, it was too late to do anything about it now.

In a few moments—which seemed more like an hour—Cliff was back.

"Get it?" Nelson demanded.

"No, there's no license on the front end of his car."

"He might be from out of state," Ted observed. "Some states don't require a front-end license."

"Well, then, we'll just have to get it from the back end," Nelson decided.

"How about it, Cliff?" asked Ted. "Can you do it, or is it too risky?"

"It's risky, all right. I'll be more exposed there, and of course he might come out any minute. I'm willing to do it, though, if you all agree."

"Sure, go ahead," said Nelson promptly, "or I'll do it myself, and you can send *me* flowers."

Cliff crept quietly forward once more. They followed his black form until he reached the front edge of the Sawyer garage, and then he was lost to them. They knew he was working his way around to the back of the car, trying to avoid exposure from the house as much as possible. They waited without speaking until they heard a faint rustle and knew that Cliff was edging his way back.

He had nearly reached them when they saw him stiffen and suddenly brace himself against the garage. They did the same, remaining absolutely motionless. They heard a click, and the quiet closing of a door, and knew a man was coming out. He came around to the driver's side of the car, which was toward the fence. They could see him in silhouette, and if there had been more light they would surely have been discovered.

But the driver unsuspectingly got into the car. He switched on the parking lights, which faintly touched the fronts of their shirts—they had not stopped to put on jackets—but apparently the driver didn't notice them. He backed out the drive, and drove off.

"No license on the rear end, either," Cliff said once they were inside again.

"Boy, you'd think he'd get picked up, driving around without a license."

"I'll bet he does have a license on most of the time," Ted remarked. "He probably takes it off just to come here."

"Yes, I think so, too," Cliff agreed. "It looked as if it'd been removed lately."

"And if that proves anything at all," said Nelson, "it at least proves he's up to no good. I'm glad we weren't wearing coats, especially heavy sports coats, or he'd surely have seen us. Or if he'd put on his bright lights we'd have been dead ducks."

"I think we're a couple of other things ahead, too," Ted added. "We know the make of car—"

"Sure, and there are only a million other cars like it in the country," put in Nelson.

"—and we all saw the man. Not well enough to identify him, I suppose, but at least we know it wasn't Mr. Sawyer." With this the others agreed. "Another thing is that I don't think he broke into the Sawyer house. He must have had a key."

"Maybe a skeleton key," suggested Cliff.

"Yes, but even then he'd probably have a set of keys he'd have to try. And from what you said I don't think he did. He seemed to walk right in. That means he's there with Mr. Sawyer's permission, at least."

"Maybe he's just a friend of Mr. Sawyer, taking care of his furnace and things while Mr. Sawyer is away," came from Cliff.

"At two-thirty in the morning?" asked Ted.

"And why doesn't he have a license plate?" Nelson objected.

That seemed to settle the matter. After further discussion, it was decided that there was little use continuing the vigil that night.

"I don't think this fellow will be back," Ted decided, "and I don't think Mr. Sawyer will be, either. This man probably knows more about Mr. Sawyer's whereabouts than we do."

"Maybe he just happened to miss him, and he'll try again tomorrow night," was Cliffs suggestion.

"Maybe. But anyway I think we'd better try to pick up a little sleep tonight."

"I'm not too sleepy," Cliff replied. "I'm used to staying up late during the holidays with my short wave. I think I'll watch for a while longer tonight. How about coming back tomorrow night?"

"Your mother'll probably be ready to toss us out by that time. But if you don't mind watching by yourself, Cliff, I'll tell you what you can do. We've got a new plug-in telephone at home, and tomorrow night I'll plug it in my room. You can call me any time during the night, in case anything comes up."

"And you can call *me* any time, Ted," Nelson added generously. "So we don't have a plug-in telephone and it wakes up the whole household, what do I care?"

"What do you make of it now, Ted?" asked Nelson on the short drive home. "Still think it might be a kidnapping?"

"No, I don't really, but I have to admit it's possible. I sure hope nothing that bad is happening to the Sawyer family."

"Me, too," said Nelson with a sigh.

CHAPTER 11

GUARD DUTY

At the office the next morning, Ted asked Mr. Dobson:

"What sort of work did Mr. Sawyer do before he came to Forestdale?"

"I don't recall now, Ted. Why?"

"Oh, I thought that perhaps he liked his earlier job better and decided to go back to it."

"I doubt if that would account for the abrupt manner in which he quit this one. But I suppose the information would be on his personnel card."

Ted took this as permission for him to consult the card, and he did so. He found that Mr. Sawyer had formerly been an accountant. There were other details, too, but Ted felt they were of no immediate interest. However, he did find what he was looking for. Mr. Sawyer had a sister living on a farm east of Forestdale—the direction in which Mr. Sawyer had been heading when Ted saw him leave town. Ted memorized the name and address carefully, and replaced the card.

Soon afterward Ted set out upon his rounds. When he examined the police blotter, one item stood out: the theft of a bolt of cloth from the dry-goods store reported early that morning. Since Ted and Mr. Dobson had anticipated something of this sort, it came as no surprise to Ted. Here was proof, if anything further was needed, that their chain of reasoning was sound.

Ought he to tell the police sergeant who had stolen this particular item? No, he decided, for he was only an employee of Mr. Dobson and it was up to the editor to decide on the action to be taken. Instead, Ted remarked:

"Is this all you've got for me?"

Sergeant Jeffers looked up suddenly. "What do you mean? This is the police blotter, and that's it."

Not wanting to mention Mr. Sawyer's name, Ted said, "I just thought maybe you had some investigations going on that weren't on the blotter yet."

"Well, of course we don't put down our suspicions, tips, anonymous calls, and things of that sort. Most of them end up in what I call our 'garbage' file. We look into them, and if anything comes of them they end up on the police blotter. What we put down are our formal complaints and arrests and investigations, which are the only things a newspaper would be interested in publishing."

Was it just his imagination, or was the sergeant's voice a bit edgy? Ted had told his friends during the night that he hadn't detected any unusual activity at the station, but now he wasn't so certain. Maybe he hadn't noticed it before because he hadn't been looking for it.

Ted thanked the sergeant, and continued on his rounds. When he returned to the office, he reported the theft to Mr. Dobson. Miss Monroe listened with amusement.

"A whole bolt of cloth? I wonder what in the world a woman would do with that?"

"Couldn't she make clothing for the children, and curtains, and things like that?" asked Ted.

"I suppose she could, but no woman would want everything made with the same pattern. I imagine that would not occur to a man. We had better not be too surprised if Mrs. Vance doesn't appear too grateful."

"We aren't sure yet that Mrs. Vance will receive it," said Ted cautiously.

"I feel quite confident of it," Mr. Dobson put in. "I think we've diagnosed this thief's method of operation, and what we've learned so far suggests that he'll run true to form. None of this is helping the newspaper's reputation any, but we'll just have to work out some sort of settlement after the contest is over."

Toward the end of the morning the telephone rang and Miss Monroe answered. Ted and Mr. Dobson caught the name "Mrs. Vance," and listened to this end of the conversation.

"Why, yes, Mrs. Vance, we're glad you liked it... No, the newspaper didn't send it, but someone may have learned about your need through the newspaper... Perhaps you could dye some of it, if you don't object to solid colors… You're very welcome. Good-by, Mrs. Vance."

Miss Monroe, smiled as she hung up. "She did receive the entire bolt. She doesn't know who brought it. It must have come by personal messenger, late last night or early this morning. She really doesn't know what to do with all forty yards of it. Of course I didn't tell her it was stolen, but I think if we have to tell her afterward she will be willing to return a good part of it."

Mr. Dobson looked very serious. "We'll have to put an immediate stop to this sort of thing, that's for sure. Ted, I don't like to take you off your regular duties, but I'm afraid there's no help for it. Today's contest window is in a jewelry shop, and I'm sure we don't want any slip-ups there. I want you to get there before Santa Claus, and watch him every minute until he's gone."

"Won't that make him suspicious? I thought what we wanted was proof."

"I think we've got all the proof we need already. Right now I want to safeguard the newspaper's reputation, prevent the store's losing any merchandise, and save Mr. Gentry from his own impulses if I can. If he grows suspicious, that's something that can't be helped."

When Ted returned from lunch, he found Nelson and Andy discussing chess-playing machines.

"No, Lulu isn't constructed to play chess, though they have machines like that. Do you play chess yourself?"

"No," Nelson replied, "though I've watched it played."

"Well, if you were an average player, a machine could probably beat you, though it doesn't play as good a game as an expert. In a chess game, the first player has a choice of twenty moves—although some of them would be foolish. His opponent also has a choice of twenty moves, making a possibility of four hundred choices for the first two moves. Then the first player may have a choice of perhaps twenty second moves, which makes eight thousand possibilities for the first three moves. You can understand why a chess machine can't see a great many moves ahead—either the possibilities would go beyond the capacity of the machine, or else it would take the machine too long a time to select its move. An expert player can see more moves ahead than a machine, one reason being that he can discard a great many foolish possibilities, while the machine must consider them all.

"A machine has other weaknesses. It can only have the skill which the designer built into it, and often there is a legitimate difference of opinion among experts as to whether one position is stronger than another. The machines now in use always capture a man if they can do so without obvious harm. This means that they will always accept an opponent's sacrifice, though they are incapable of making a sacrifice themselves. A machine can't vary its strategy, although an expert might play one kind of game against an impatient player and another against a cautious player. And a machine of this sort doesn't learn from experience. If it makes a poor move in a certain situation, it will continue to make that same poor move in the same situation."

"I wonder if it would feel worse to lose to a machine or to an expert player?" asked Nelson with a laugh.

"What's the difference?" Ted chimed in. "When you lose to the machine, you're really losing to the designer of the machine, and he had to be an expert."

Nelson had a round of calls to make, and on his way he dropped Ted off at the jewelry shop.

"Too bad Lulu can't solve our problem for us," he commented. "If Lulu's such a big brain, why can't she tell us what's happening to Mr. Sawyer?"

"Maybe it's our fault for not asking her the right questions."

"You know, I'm sort of losing my respect for Lulu. She's not really a brain. It seems to me that she's just a big sorting machine—she can sort out all the possible answers till she comes to the one you want, and she can do it faster because of her electronic system. But when you ask Lulu to solve a problem, you're really asking the operator to solve the problem. He sets it up, and then lets Lulu sort it out for him."

"Well, don't get sore about it," Ted kidded him in parting. *"I'm not jealous of Lulu."*

Ted went inside fifteen minutes before Santa Claus was due. Soon afterward he arrived, coming in the rear entrance and passing through to the front of the store. He gave Ted a friendly nod, but if he wondered what Ted was doing there, he asked no questions.

Besides his pack, Santa had brought an armful of books with him. He set the pack down, opened it, and took out some small boxes of little presents for the children who crowded around him. Although his pack seemed inexhaustible, the supply of Santa Claus books was not, and as the pile diminished Mr. Gentry said: "Ted, would you mind going out to my car and bringing in another stack? I've had to leave my reindeer home today," he explained to the children. "I'm resting them for Christmas."

His job was to keep an eye on Santa Claus, but Ted decided it ought to be safe enough to leave for just a minute. With that crowd of children about him, and a scattering of adults on the outskirts, it didn't seem possible that Santa could stir from his chair while Ted was gone. He hurried outside through the back, quickly procured the books, and almost ran back in. Santa was still sitting in the same position.

"Thank you, Ted. Now here, children—" and Mr. Gentry launched into a little anecdote about his adventures. It was bedlam, but still the hour passed swiftly and pleasantly enough. Some of the children would have liked Santa to remain longer, but he assured them that his presence was urgently required elsewhere if he were to do an effective job of toy delivery on Christmas Eve, and they allowed him to go. Ted followed him at a little distance to the back door. He waited in the doorway until he saw Mr. Gentry's car drive off. He then left the store and returned directly to the newspaper office, where he reported to Mr. Dobson.

"He was never alone, then, Ted?"

"Only for half a minute or so, while I went out back for some more books, but he had twenty or thirty people around him at the time. Mr. Hartley was watching, too. I suppose his most expensive things were locked up, but he does have some unlocked glass cases, and probably didn't want anyone to get any ideas."

"You say Mr. Gentry came in through the back. Could he have taken anything then?"

Ted shook his head. "There's nothing there in the narrow passageway. Anyway, I could see him from the time the door opened until he came through to the front."

Mr. Dobson seemed satisfied. "Well, anyway, this is one time we won't have to worry about anything missing. It was beginning to wear on my conscience."

"Then I suppose I'm to watch Mr. Gentry tomorrow afternoon, too?"

"Thursday? No, Ted, I think it will be up to Miss Monroe or me to take care of it then, If you and Nelson are going to take over the circulation Thursday night, I can hardly expect you to work all day, too. You'll have the afternoon off. I wish I could give you the morning off, but you know that Thursday morning is one of our busiest times. You needn't come in Friday morning, however."

During the evening he thought about Cliff, who was no doubt sitting up to watch Mr. Sawyer's house through most of the night. He wanted to call him, but thought better of it, for if Cliff should answer within hearing of his parents, they might ask questions. Ted was determined to keep the matter as quiet as he could. During the activity of the day he had very nearly forgotten Mr. Sawyer's problem, but now it returned with full force. Could it really be a kidnapping, and if not, what was it? Were they doing the wisest thing? Should they give up their vigil and the slight chance they might be discovered? Or, on the other hand, were they interfering too little, and might better notify the police at once? If things turned out badly, they would feel guilty, and wish they had done the opposite thing.

Ted remembered to take the upstairs telephone into his own room and plug it in. He then muffled it with a pillow so it wouldn't arouse his mother if it rang. He retired before ten-thirty, and fell asleep almost at once. At three o'clock the telephone began to ring.

CHAPTER 12

A BAD GUESS

For a moment Ted was confused, thinking the bell was the alarm clock, and he fumbled about for it in the darkness. But he speedily oriented himself, and recovered the receiver.

"Hello?" he said cautiously.

"Ted, something's going on in back. Mr. Sawyer's there, and the other man. They're both in the house now."

"Did Mr. Sawyer come with him?"

"No, he came first in his own car. Then about half an hour later the other car drove up—the same one we saw last night."

"How long have they been in the house?"

"About fifteen minutes. I'm wondering—do you think maybe Mr. Sawyer's in any danger?"

Ted considered carefully. "It doesn't seem very likely. He came first, and alone. It looks as though he must have had an appointment with the man. And I don't think this helps the kidnapping theory much. Kidnapers would hardly show their faces to the father of the victim."

"Maybe this man's just an intermediary."

"I suppose that's possible," Ted agreed. "Well, I don't know what we can do—"

"Wait a minute, Ted. I think they're coming outside again. I can't see from this window. Hang on while I sneak upstairs again and see what's coming off."

Ted waited, and a couple of minutes later Cliff returned to the phone.

"The other car just drove off."

"Then Mr. Sawyer's still in the house?"

"Yes, I think so. Anyway, his car's still here."

Cliff waited, as though he hoped Ted would have something to suggest, but Ted could think of nothing to do.

"I don't see how we can interfere, the way things are now."

"You know, Ted," said Cliff seriously, "I've sort of had this kidnapping bug on my mind, but it could be something else. Even good men sometimes turn bad in a crisis. Maybe Mr. Sawyer is mixed up in a shady deal of some sort, and we ought to notify the police."

"That could be, but his past reputation is really all we've got to go on. And if it should be a kidnapping, I think we ought to respect Mr. Sawyer's wishes in the matter. I know I wouldn't want to take the responsibility for spreading the news around."

"Then what are we going to *do?*" asked Cliff plaintively, as though not doing something was the worst of all possible courses.

"I did find out one thing, Cliff. Mr. Sawyer has a sister on a farm near here, and it's just possible that's where the family is hiding out. Nelson and I have this afternoon off. I think maybe the three of us can get out to the farm and somehow try to find out. If Tommy's there, at least we'll know it isn't a kidnapping."

"Well, all right," Cliff agreed grudgingly, "but I hate putting things off any longer than we have to."

After arranging to meet with Cliff at noon the next day, Ted hung up. As long as Mr. Sawyer was back in town and apparently moving about freely, the situation did not seem quite so black as they had imagined it. However, it remained as puzzling as ever, and after considering every possible alternative, Ted finally gave it up and went to sleep again.

When he arrived at the office at his usual time, he found Mr. Dobson in a disturbed frame of mind.

"Ted," he began without preliminary, "I've just had a call from Mr. Hartley. He tells me that a wrist watch was stolen from his store yesterday!"

Ted was dumfounded. "But—I was watching him nearly every minute. Even when I went out the back he was so surrounded that I didn't see how he could move from his chair. Is Mr. Hartley going to report it to the police?"

"I think he will, Ted. He called to ask me what I thought, since he didn't want to do anything to cast reflections on our contest, but I told him I didn't have any objection. Of course he doesn't suspect Mr. Gentry particularly. In all that confused throng it could be almost anyone. I wish we could get through the last three days of the contest.

Saturday is Compton's butcher shop's day, so he shouldn't find very much to take there. I think, Ted, that from now on it's up to me to take over the job of watching Mr. Gentry."

He added, as Ted looked disappointed, "This doesn't mean that you've done a bad job, Ted, or that I think I can do any better. It's just that I think the situation is growing in seriousness, and I no longer care to delegate the responsibility to anyone else. Maybe I made a mistake when I didn't report the whole thing to the police right at the start, but I wanted to help both the newspaper and Mr. Gentry, if I could. The trouble is that when you try to help a person, you often run into this same difficulty: you find that the causes of the problem run much deeper than you at first believed. I thought that Mr. Gentry was just a pretend Santa Claus who decided he wanted to help people. But the manner in which that watch was stolen, even while you were on the scene, suggests to me that Mr. Gentry must be an old hand at this business."

The usual Thursday-morning bustle kept Ted on the jump, just as it did everyone else on the staff. At noon Nelson picked up Cliff and him. None of the three had eaten lunch, and they stopped at a hamburger stand where they could eat and plot their strategy at the same time.

"I think it's important to know whether Tommy is out at the farm," Ted pointed out, "but I'm not so sure that I ought to get mixed up in it. If I'm recognized, it might appear to Mr. Sawyer that the newspaper is trying to track him down."

"I work for the newspaper, too, I think," Nelson added.

"Well, I don't mind doing it myself," Cliff stated, "but how are we going to work it? Isn't there some way we could keep a watch on the farm from a distance and see who's there?"

"I don't think that will work." Ted shook his head. "Look at the weather. You can't count on Tommy's being allowed outside to play on a day like this. And if we did see someone about his size from a distance, we might not be able to tell for sure who it was, even with binoculars. Seeing Mr. or Mrs. Sawyer, of course, wouldn't prove anything at all. They could still be there while Tommy was missing. I think the only way is for you to go right up to the house. Do you think Tommy would recognize you?"

"No, I don't think so. I've never had much to do with him, and anyway he hasn't seen me since September. Another thing is that people dress so much more heavily in winter that about the only way you can recognize them is by what they're wearing. If I put on Nel's loud jacket, I've got an idea that Mrs. Sawyer might not recognize me, either."

"What about Mr. Sawyer?" asked Nelson.

Cliff shook his head negatively. "I don't think I could do anything to fool him. He used to umpire our Class D games, and he knows me pretty well. I don't think Mr. Sawyer will be out at the farm, though. His car was still in the garage when I left. I know because I checked."

"Why don't we do it this way?" Ted suggested. "We'll all drive out to the farm, but just Cliff will go in, since he's probably the only one who could recognize Tommy for sure anyway. He can have a package with him, and pretend he's come to the wrong place with it. By the time he asks a few questions he'll probably be able to find out what we want to know."

No one had any better idea than this, so it was agreed on. They drove back to Cliff's, and he did up a package which looked as though it had just come from a store.

"What name shall I put on it?" he asked.

"No name—just a blank label," Ted instructed him. "We'll have to find a real name so it'll look authentic. Sometimes those farm families know everybody for miles around."

Cliff exchanged coats with Nelson, and they set out. It was a drive of some twelve or thirteen miles. As they reached the proper crossroad, Ted said:

"What direction are we supposed to go now?"

"South," Cliff responded.

"Then let's go north," Ted ordered.

"Why?" Nelson demanded.

"Because we want to pick up an authentic name off one of these mailboxes. Then Cliff can pretend he simply turned the wrong way."

They soon found a name they thought would do, far enough away from the other farm so that the two families probably had no neighborly intimacy.

"But they could still be close friends," Nelson argued. "They might go to the same church, or be in the same grange, or something like that."

"Well, we'll just have to chance it," Cliff decided. "Anyway, there won't be any great harm done, just so they don't check on it before I can get out."

Before reaching the farm, Ted and Nelson changed into the back seat. There, leaning far back, they could not readily be seen through the side windows. Cliff now took the wheel, and came to a stop on the main road in front of the farm. The house was set some distance back from the road, so that it would be natural for visitors to drive in, but they couldn't chance that. Cliff observed the mailbox.

"How can I pretend to make a mistake, when the name is printed plainly on the box?" he complained.

"Tell them you thought they might have just moved in," Ted directed. "Pretend you're a stranger around here yourself. Act a little bit stupid."

"Just act natural," Nelson advised him.

Package in hand, Cliff trudged toward the house through the light snow. Ted and Nelson watched anxiously through the edge of the car window, making sure that they would not be noticed from the house. They saw Cliff knock at the door, and a moment later it was opened and he went inside.

"Anyway, he got in," Nelson observed. "That's half the battle. If Tommy's anywhere around, he'll come prancing into the kitchen to see who's come. That's the way kids always do."

A few minutes later the kitchen door opened again, and Cliff reappeared. It was slow walking, and he made no sign to them, lest someone be watching from the house.

"Well, that's out," said Cliff, as he climbed into the car and slammed the door after him. "Tommy was there, and happy as a lark."

"Did he recognize you?" asked Ted.

"No, but he did ask my name. I told him I was Jack Frost, Santa Claus's helper, but I don't know whether he believed it or not."

"Then you didn't see Mr. or Mrs. Sawyer?" Nelson questioned.

"No, but I did hear someone else in the house. I talked with Mrs.—what's that name on the mailbox?—Boscome. She was very considerate and helpful. I don't think she suspected anything."

"It could still be a kidnapping *threat,*" Nelson pointed out. "Maybe the family came out here as a precaution."

"No, I gave up on that idea as soon as I saw what the situation was. Tommy was running around just as he normally would. If he'd been threatened, I think they would have been more careful with him, especially when someone came to the door."

"If they wanted to hide out, I think they would have picked a better place than this," Ted added. "We found them too easily, so I imagine a kidnaper could have done it, too. Maybe they just came out here to spend the holidays."

"Then why did they leave town at five o'clock in the morning?" Nelson persisted. "It wasn't as though they had a long trip and wanted to get an early start."

"Maybe Mr. Sawyer had to get them out here before he went on to his regular work."

"It doesn't look to me like Mr. Sawyer is very much interested in work right now," Nelson retorted. "Look at the way he quit the newspaper, the hours he's keeping, and the people he's been meeting. Anyway, he's always regulated his own hours pretty well, so why should he be in such a hurry to get to work so early in the morning? He deals in construction materials, and that line's always slack at this time of year. I think he's got something else on his mind besides work."

"Well, what'll we do?" Cliff wanted to know. "This has gotten exciting. I hate to give up now."

"I suppose you can keep on watching his house, if you want to," said Ted slowly. "But I don't know what good that's going to do. We know he's been getting a late visitor or visitors, but we don't know who they are or what they're up to."

"I guess we'd better try to get a little shut-eye ourselves," Nelson commented, "as long as we're going to be up all night. Is Mr. White coming in tonight, Ted?"

"No, I told him I thought we could handle it ourselves. The addressing machine is the trickiest part, but we watched him, and I think we can manage it. If not, we can give him a call, or let it wait till morning."

They felt a little disappointed as they reached the town limits. While they were glad to know Tommy was safe, still they felt the afternoon had been rather a waste, as far as solving the case was concerned.

CHAPTER 13

A VISITOR FOR LULU

Ted and Nelson reported for work at seven-thirty. Mr. White had finished by that time and gone home. The big printing room was silent, and the hanging lights cast grotesque shadows against the walls.

"This place is eerie, when you're all alone," Nelson observed. "I don't suppose there're any stories about ghosts hanging around the printing presses?"

"I never heard of any, unless it's the ghost of John Peter Zenger. He might get annoyed if anyone tried to tamper with the freedom of the press. But he wouldn't hang around here. Mr. Dobson does exactly as he pleases with the *Town Crier,* so I guess there's no question of freedom. If he makes any mistakes, they're his own."

"All well and good, Ted, but don't you think Mr. Dobson is suppressing this Santa Claus story?"

"No, Nel, I don't. Thefts in shops at this season are common, and he didn't feel they were important enough to use before."

"But this is different—a Santa Claus who steals to help poor people. That's a good story, isn't it?"

"A good human-interest story, maybe. I wouldn't call it a news story."

"What's the difference?" Nelson wanted to know.

Ted smiled. "Oh, I'd say it's a story in which the climax *doesn't* come at the beginning, like most newspaper stories. Of course that's only one of its characteristics."

"Well, how do you know this Santa Claus story is a human-interest and not a news story?"

"Because what's happening isn't of any great importance. It's only the character of the persons concerned that makes it at all important. If you want any proof about it, all I can say is that the *News-Record* isn't printing anything about these thefts, either."

"Maybe the *News-Record* doesn't know about the thefts, with Ken Kutler in jail."

"Oh, they must have somebody checking the police records. I know our police keep a file on important items from nearby towns, for criminals don't stop at boundaries. I wonder how Ken's enjoying jail? I don't wish him any bad luck, but I'm glad he isn't around breathing down my neck. I don't think our Santa Claus story is big enough to interest him, but—"

"But maybe Mr. Sawyer's trouble is," said Nelson quickly. "Maybe it would be a good thing to have Ken around. I bet we'd get some action on that. I've been wondering, Ted—don't you think maybe it's time for us to go to the police, now that we know it isn't a kidnapping case?"

"What have we got to report?" asked Ted, turning his hands up hopelessly. "He quit his job, but that's no crime. He's receiving a late visitor. Well, that could be perfectly legitimate, too. Maybe they're planning some big business deal."

"Then the first order of business ought to be to buy some new license plates," Nelson concluded. "Even if they just got lost and the end of the year is almost here—they don't have to be *that* stingy, do they?"

Since they were more familiar with their work than they had been on Monday evening, they were able to handle it with greater efficiency. On the other hand, Mr. White's absence meant there was no one handy they could run to with their questions. Since the addressing machine was the trickiest and least urgent part of their work, they decided to leave that till last, and to concentrate on meeting the train and bus schedules out of town. With this in mind, they worked at a steady clip, and took satisfaction in watching the bundled and properly labeled stacks of papers piling up against the wall.

"Think we'll make it?" asked Nelson, stopping for a breather and consulting the large clock on the wall.

"With some to spare," Ted returned, pleased with the way things were going. It was nearly twelve o'clock, and they hadn't struck a hitch yet.

"Do we have to do this next *Monday* night?" asked Nelson with a sudden thought. "That's Christmas night!"

"No, I don't think so. There'll be a paper Tuesday morning, but it'll be of smaller size, and Mr. Dobson's getting it set up well in advance. He doesn't want anybody to work on Christmas."

The rest of the night went fairly smoothly, except for one hitch. When it came to using the addressing machine, they found a number of address plates which had been set aside for some reason. It wasn't clear whether these persons' subscriptions had expired, or whether the plates had been set apart for some other reason. The number involved was small, so that it seemed silly to telephone Mr. White at that hour of the night.

"What'll we do about them?" asked Nelson.

"I'll leave a note for Mr. Dobson. It won't be much work to bundle up the extra papers, if they're supposed to go."

The bus and train schedules were met, the boys made their out-of-town circuit, and then delivered all the bundles to the local carriers before the required time. They returned to the printing shop to clean up, satisfied that they had accomplished a good night's work.

"Well, that seems to be that," said Ted, straightening up with an air of everything done.

"What about that note for Mr. Dobson?" Nelson reminded him.

"Oh, that. I'll dash it off, and then off to home, food, and bed."

He quickly wrote the note, then went into the front office, switched on the light, and put the note on Mr. Dobson's desk. He wasn't sure exactly what impulse caused him to look around the office. Something about the room seemed different. Maybe it was just that he was unaccustomed to seeing it at night, he thought, and was about to switch off the light when a detail of possible significance caught his eye.

"Nelson, come in here," he called.

"What's up, Ted?" asked Nelson, hurrying into the room.

"That—over there. Lulu's canvas cover."

"What's the matter with it? It looks all right to me."

"No, it isn't. It's on sideways."

"So what? The machine's *almost* square. It fits almost as well that way as it does the other."

"I know, but I'm pretty sure Andy put it on the right way. You almost always would, if you're familiar with the machine. It's the stranger who wouldn't know, or wouldn't think it made any difference."

"That doesn't prove anything, Ted. If Andy didn't do it, maybe Mr. Dobson or Miss Monroe had some reason for taking the cover off the machine this afternoon."

"I suppose that could be," Ted answered slowly. Then his eyes turned toward the door, and almost unconsciously Nelson followed his gaze. There were slight traces of moisture on the floor near it, as though the snow brought in on someone's feet had not yet quite melted.

"Did we bring that in?" asked Nelson, lowering his voice.

"How could we? It's been hours since we've been near the front door. It would have melted by now, if we had."

Since Ted only had a key for the front door, they had come in that way. But it was easier to load the car from the rear door, and they had used the key hanging on the wall of the printing shop. Until just now they hadn't returned to the front office. Ted tried the door, but it was still locked.

"The trail seems to be leading over that way," Nelson observed.

"Yes. Right toward Lulu."

"Well, what do you know? Lulu having a visitor at this hour, and all the time I thought she was a lady." Then he looked worried. "You don't think somebody damaged Lulu, do you, Ted?"

Ted took off the cover and switched on the machine. As far as he could tell, Lulu seemed all right. Yet he was more than ever convinced that someone had come into the office for the purpose of doing or learning something about the machine.

"Look around, Ted," Nelson urged him. "It might be just an ordinary robbery. Can you tell if there's anything missing?"

There was no safe in the office, since Mr. Dobson dealt chiefly by check. Miss Monroe did keep some petty cash and postage stamps on hand, along with the check book. Ted tried the drawer of her desk where these were kept, but it was locked, and apparently there had been no attempt to force it. He looked through the other drawers of the two desks, and he saw no indication that anyone had rummaged through them.

"No robbery," Ted decided. "It must have been Lulu. Now I wonder what anybody would want with her?"

"What about the contest? Who's got the answers, Ted?"

"There are only two sets of answers, I think. Andy has one, and Mr. Dobson has the other. But you can bet your boots they don't leave the list lying around the office. That would be: the same thing as leaving a thousand-dollar bill lying around, and I don't know many people who do that. In fact, I don't know any."

"Well, what about Lulu? Is there any way somebody could get the answers from her?"

"I don't know very much about the way she works, but that doesn't sound possible to me. The way I understand it, Andy's going to fix up a card with the proper answers, and another card for each of the contestants. Then Lulu will pick out the cards which most closely resemble the answer card. But without the answer card, I don't see what anybody would have to gain by fooling around with the machine."

"What if he broke the machine so it couldn't judge the contest?"

"Then we'd have to do it all by hand. It'd be more work, but it wouldn't be any great catastrophe."

"Well, how about tampering with the contest entries?"

"It's a little early to be worrying about that, isn't it? None of the entries will come in till after the contest ends, and that's next Saturday."

They seemed to have eliminated any possibility that the intruder was concerned about the contest, but they were at a loss to explain the strange visit in any other fashion. As they stood considering the dilemma, the telephone rang. With a grim look at Nelson, Ted went to answer.

"Hello?" he said questioningly.

"Ted?" It was Cliff's voice, which was a relief to Ted.

"Yes? What's up?"

"I just wanted to tell you. Mr. Sawyer had a visitor—that same man, I think. After he left, Mr. Sawyer went out. That was more than an hour ago. I tried to call you about six times, but you were out each time."

"Has he returned yet?"

"Yes, he wasn't long. About fifteen minutes, I think. The funny thing is that when he went out he was carrying something big in his arms, like a roll of wrapping paper. And when he came back he didn't have it any more, unless he left it in his car."

Ted was beginning to grow excited. "How soon after he left did you telephone here, Cliff?"

"Oh, right away. A minute or two."

"Then how soon did you call after that?"

"Not very soon. I figured you must be out making deliveries, and there wasn't any use calling too soon. Anyway, I was interested in watching. Right after he came back I called you again."

"Well, I'm glad you did it that way, Cliff, because we know where Mr. Sawyer went. He came here, right down to the office."

"You sure about that, Ted?" asked Cliff, also growing excited.

"It must have been. We know somebody was here. The front door wasn't tampered with, and Mr. Sawyer has a key. Besides, he'd know better than anybody about our delivery schedules, and how long we'd be out."

"Well, I'll be calcified. What do you suppose was in that package?"

"I don't know. I don't see anything around here that would account for it. We know where he went, but we still don't know why."

CHAPTER 14

SOU'WESTERN

Ted and Nelson arrived at the newspaper office shortly before one o'clock on Friday, just in time to catch the end of Andy's demonstration. It was clear that Lulu was still in good working order, so the intruder couldn't have damaged her in any way. Or if that had been Mr. Sawyer's intention, apparently he had been scared off.

Andy seemed in a communicative mood, and showed the boys a few operations on Lulu. Then he gave them the chance to try it for themselves. Although they could not hope to arrive at Andy's competence in such a short time, they were beginning to get a better understanding of the machine.

"Yes, Lulu's really quite a girl," said Andy, almost with affection. "There isn't much she can't do, as long as you understand her."

"I'll bet she doesn't know the most important event of each of the Chinese dynasties," said Nelson critically. "That's what stumped me on our last history test."

"What did you put down?" asked Ted.

"I said for each one, 'Extended the Great Wall.'"

"How did you make out?"

"Well, I passed."

Andy laughed, then returned to talking about Lulu. "It's true she has her limitations. This particular machine can only remember numbers, not words. Also, your instructions must be clear and within her capacity. What do you suppose would happen if you gave her contradicting instructions?"

"She'd have a nervous breakdown?" Nelson suggested.

"Not quite. She's a more sedate creature than that. But let's try it. Now on this card I'll ask Lulu to remember a number and forget it at the same time. Let's see what she does."

The card was fed into the machine, and to the boys' surprise and delight the machine's calculations came to a halt while it printed a line across the paper:

Please check your data, operator.

At this so-human comment the boys and Andy laughed. Then they talked about the machine and the contest for a few minutes longer.

"We're going to hate to see you leave, Andy," Ted remarked. "You and Lulu are almost part of the newspaper family."

"Oh, you'll be seeing plenty of both of us next week, when we grade the contest entries. I hope I don't run into any headaches over that."

Then Andy left, not because he was particularly busy himself, but because he realized they were. He hadn't said anything more about going to college, so either he was making no plans, or else he was keeping them strictly to himself.

Nelson also left to pick up and deliver more Make a Wish donations. When Ted was alone with Mr. Dobson, he explained about the night's adventure.

"Did Mr. Sawyer ever show much interest in Lulu, Mr. Dobson?"

"Why, yes, I believe he did. He was here when the machine first came in, and stood around asking Andy questions while he was getting it set up."

Mr. Dobson had something to report, too. "I called the shoe store this morning, to see if there were any thefts yesterday. I thought it possible that Mr. Gentry had managed to elude me, just the way he did you."

"What did they say?"

"They couldn't tell me. They said they have some temporary clerks there, and being inexperienced, they may have put some things away in the wrong places. It would take a complete inventory to check the matter, and naturally they're too busy for that now."

Mr. Dobson wanted to go out on guard duty again, Ted had his rounds to make, and Miss Monroe also had a few necessary errands. In order that someone should be at the office at all times, it was arranged that Ted should go first, and try to get back about the time Mr.

Dobson had to leave, or soon after. Then Miss Monroe could go out, and Ted would stay on duty till Mr. Dobson returned.

After returning to the office, Ted found a new batch of thank-you notes to copy. There was also his regular typing, and with proofreading chores and answering telephone calls, he was kept quite busy. Late in the afternoon, shortly after Mr. Dobson's return, Nelson came in.

"Mr. Dobson," he addressed the editor, "I wasn't able to deliver that steam iron. The family's moved away—out to Westover. Do you want me to deliver it anyway?"

"Well, I would like to have it delivered, but that's pretty far away. Is it too far for you?"

"Oh, no, I don't mind doing it."

"Well, then, I'd appreciate it if you did."

"Coming along for the ride, Ted?" asked Nelson, for he had promised to drive Ted home.

"Yes, I guess so. I'm just about finished here."

Out on the open road, Nelson remarked, "You know, Ted, Westover isn't too far from Sou'western. You want to stop off there?"

"Think we'll have time?"

"If we want to take time. You said you were anxious to go to Sou'western before next week. Mr. Dobson will have to figure out what he's going to do about Mr. Gentry by then. I guess Christmas isn't so much fun, if you know you'll have to arrest Santa Claus right afterward. It's a shame, too, because he seems like such a good-hearted guy."

"Goodhearted with other people's property, at least. But I'm willing to stop if you are. If we could locate some relatives of Mr. Gentry's, it might help. Perhaps they could suggest something."

They had no trouble finding the home of the person who had moved, and Nelson delivered the steam iron. The additional ten miles to Sou'western were quickly covered.

"Now what do we do?" asked Nelson, as they entered the outskirts.

"Let's see if they have a library. If they do, they may have a last-year's directory, and we can find out where Mr. and Mrs. Malcolm lived. If we can find the house, the people living there may know something about them. If not, the neighbors may."

"From the size of this burg, everybody ought to know everything about everybody," was Nelson's answer.

They found the library and the old directory, and from this quickly learned the address. But at the house they found Ted was mistaken in one respect.

"I'm sorry, but we never knew Mr. and Mrs. Malcolm," the woman answering their ring informed them. "We moved out here and bought the house shortly after the accident. I believe Mr. Dressier next door may be able to tell you what you want to know. He seems to have been a good friend of theirs."

The boys thanked her, and went next door. Mr. Dressier, having learned the nature of their errand, asked them in.

"Yes, I knew the Malcolms quite well," he assured them. "They were very fine people, and news of the accident came as a great shock to me. I believe they were off on a visit to see their son, Tony, who was at school, and that the accident occurred on the return trip."

"Then there was a son?" asked Ted in surprise, this possibility not having occurred to him. "Do you know what happened to him?"

"No, but I suppose he stayed on at school. What else was there for him to do? I believe he did return to Sou'western briefly to help with the closing up of the house. I would have been glad to assist him, but he didn't ask me, so that actually I didn't get to see him at all. But I heard that he was pretty broken up over the accident."

"There were no other relatives?"

"None at all, so far as I know. He put his affairs into the hands of an attorney, to arrange for the sale of the house and so on, and left soon afterward. I suppose he didn't want to miss any more school than necessary, and hard work is often a good antidote for grief. It was probably the best thing he could do—certainly better than moping about an empty house that could only remind him of his double loss."

"Mr. Gentry wasn't a relative, then?"

"No, I understood he wasn't. He was an old friend of Mr. Malcolm's, reaching back to the days before he was married. But they seemed to accept him just like one of the family. I remember when Tony was just a little boy, Mr. Gentry would read to him, and when Tony got a little older, Mr. Gentry would take out a baseball glove and help him practice his pitching."

"Mr. Gentry wasn't married?"

"No, or at least not during the period that I knew him. I suppose that not having a family of his own made him virtually adopt the Malcolm family. Not that he was here too much. He was an important businessman, tall, alert, ambitious, energetic, mature. I believe his work required him to travel a great deal, but I once heard him say that getting back to Sou'western was like coming home."

"He had no relatives of his own?"

"None that I ever heard of."

"What about the accident?" said Nelson, speaking for the first time. "How did it happen?"

"Well, I believe the police theory was that Mr. Gentry fell asleep at the wheel. They had been driving a long way, and it was night, so I suppose he was tired. Somehow I've never felt that was the real explanation, myself. Usually when a driver falls asleep at the wheel he is alone. If he has passengers with him and starts nodding, usually they notice and do something about it."

"Unless they are sleepy, too," Ted observed.

"Yes, I suppose that's possible. But I've felt it happened differently. I think they were late and anxious to get home, so they took a short cut on an unfamiliar road. Somehow this must have confused Mr. Gentry, and he drove the car off the road. However, I can't see that it makes any difference. Did you boys say that you knew Mr. Gentry?"

"We thought we did, but I'm not so sure," Nelson put in. "The way you've described him doesn't sound much like the person we know. He looks sort of old and stooped and gentle, and probably tired or worn out."

"In his Santa-Claus outfit," Ted added. "We've never seen him in anything else."

"No, that doesn't sound very much like the Mr. Gentry I knew, but I suppose he *is* growing older, just like all the rest of us. The accident must have had an effect on him, too—losing his best friends, being injured himself."

"Yes, I don't think there's any question that it's the same man," said Ted, frowning, "and that the accident did change him. It's just that he seems all alone and rather forlorn, and we were wondering if there was any way we could help him."

"That's rather a new twist, helping Santa Claus," said Mr. Dressier with a laugh. "But it's a generous thought. I don't think money is any problem with him. As a successful engineer for a good many years, he must have been able to put aside a good portion of his income. But I suppose his problem is the same as everyone's: finding the kind of friends who really matter to you."

Ted got to his feet, and Nelson followed his example.

"Well, thank you, Mr. Dressier. You've been very helpful."

"I'm glad I could help a little. It's been a pleasure talking to you boys. Merry Christmas."

"Merry Christmas," they responded, and started toward the door.

As they were about to get into the car Mr. Dressier called after them once more: "Say, boys, if you really want to help Mr. Gentry, I know something you can do for him."

"What's that?" asked Ted.

"Find Tony Malcolm for him," said Mr. Dressier, and closed the door.

CHAPTER 15

THREE WISHES

It was Nelson's suggestion that he and Ted meet again at Cliff's that evening to see if there was anything further going on at Mr. Sawyer's. Cliff consented by telephone, but when they arrived and went up to his room they found him impatient.

"I've been watching the house, but what good is it doing us? I see Mr. Sawyer going in and out. I see another man going in and out. So what? How are we ever going to find anything out that way?"

"Is he there now?" asked Ted.

Cliff motioned toward the window. There was a light on, but apparently only one. "He is, but his family isn't back yet."

"And that other man?"

"I haven't seen anything of him tonight."

"Then why don't we go over there?" said Nelson.

"What do you mean? Go over where?" Cliff retorted.

"Why, to Mr. Sawyer's house."

"You mean go right up to his door and ring?" asked Cliff incredulously. He turned to Ted. "This guy's crazy, isn't he?"

"Mm, I don't know," said Ted thoughtfully. "Maybe it's not such a crazy idea. We've eliminated the idea of kidnapping, so I don't think we have to be as careful as we thought. Besides, I think we've got a legitimate reason to interfere now. If he wants to quit his job and conduct some business arrangement of his own, that's his concern—probably. But when he's no longer employed by the *Town Crier* and still comes sneaking into the office at the dead of night, then that concerns us."

"Okay, so we go over there. You think he'll tell us anything?"

"I don't know, and we won't till we try it."

"Sure, let's go," Nelson urged. "We're not afraid of him. I mean I don't think we are. Are we?"

"All right," Cliff agreed. "I'm willing, if you fellows are. I can't see myself just sitting here for another week, wondering what's going on. But it's pretty late. You think this is the best time?"

"He's still up," Nelson pointed out.

"Yes," Ted added, "and it's still early for his night-time visitor, so maybe we'll catch him betwixt and between."

With the decision made, they felt unexpectedly relieved. This at least was action after a long period of doing nothing. And even if Mr. Sawyer didn't tell them everything, they felt that his attitude would at least reveal something to them.

"The neighbors won't see us now," Cliff observed, as they approached Mr. Sawyer's home from the pathway between the garages and the fence. "That's just as well. No use making a big stir."

"He must be in the kitchen," Nelson pointed out, indicating the light coming through a back window, "and I sure hope he's alone. I don't think we ought to walk into anything."

"Easy enough to find out," Cliff retorted, starting over toward the window.

"Hey!" Ted cautioned him in a low voice. "I don't think we ought to go around looking in people's windows."

"Then people ought to keep their blinds closed," Cliff responded, and Ted had no time to object further. Cliff stretched up to peer through the high window. Suddenly they saw him give a gesture of surprise, and hurry quietly back toward them.

"What's the matter?" Nelson inquired.

"Wow! Money! Scads and scads of it," Cliff informed them.

"Money?" Ted questioned him. "What's he doing with it?"

"Counting it, I suppose. He's got it arranged in little stacks. Well, we still going to ring?"

"Sure, why not?" Nelson countered. "I'm more anxious than ever to see what he's up to."

Ted rang the bell at the side door. There was a lapse of about a minute, while someone seemed to be scurrying around inside. Then the hall light was switched on, and Mr. Sawyer opened the door. He seemed surprised to see them, but whether he was very unhappy about it was impossible to tell.

"Oh, that you, Ted?" he said questioningly.

"Yes, Mr. Sawyer." Ted felt he must explain their errand. "Someone entered the *Town Crier* office last night while we were out, and we wondered if you knew anything about it."

Although he hadn't exactly accused Mr. Sawyer, the implication was clear. As the man still seemed undecided, Cliff blurted out, "I don't suppose that had anything to do with all that money you had stacked up on the table."

"You saw that, too?" He seemed to be trying to make up his mind, and the boys wondered if he would try to deny everything and send them on their way. But apparently he felt they already knew so much he had better make some sort of explanation to them.

"Come on. Come on in," he invited them, cordially enough, and they stepped into the hallway. From the kitchen he procured a bundle of bills, and flipped through it. They could tell that the money was chiefly of small denomination.

"How much is there?" Nelson questioned.

"Seven hundred fifty dollars—with twelve hundred fifty more supposed to follow, which I'll never get. I never hated any money so much in my life. You must believe that I didn't do this for the money—even though I know it's going to be hard to get anybody to believe that. But come on into the living room where we'll be more comfortable, and I'll tell you about it."

As the boys advanced into the darkened living room, he returned the money to its place of concealment. Then he joined them, switched on a light, and they all sat down.

"It has something to do with Lulu, doesn't it?" Ted began.

The former circulation manager looked surprised once more. "You discovered that? You're perfectly right, but that's not where my story begins. I'm going to be completely frank with you, and tell you some things I've never told anyone except my wife. A few years ago I was with the army of occupation in Europe. While there I became involved with a black-market operation. I was never caught, but if I had been, I would probably have been given a dishonorable discharge, at the very least.

"My connection was with a man I shall call Kimbill, because that was the name he gave me, though I'm pretty sure now that wasn't his real name. He was an American, though not in the army. Believe me, he was in much deeper than I was. I only operated on the fringes, so to speak, and excused myself by thinking that I was only stretching a few points to help out some friends. I never made much out of it myself, and the little I got, I paid for with worry. Never again, I told myself. When I'm out of this, I'm through—and I meant it.

"Eventually I returned to the United States and was discharged, and I think that ever since then I've lived up to the promise I made myself. I didn't see Kimbill again until about a month ago. He had a new scheme in mind, and naturally, since I'd helped him once before, he thought I'd be willing to help him again. His scheme sounded incredible to me, but he showed me an article in a small technical journal which seemed to bear him out. The article concerned an electronic machine nicknamed Lulu. The article mentioned that the machine had cost an incredible sum—half a million dollars I think it was—to construct, that the inner workings were still highly secret, and that there were rivals who would be willing to pay immense sums for those secrets.

"When the machine arrived at the *Town Crier* office, I questioned Markum closely about it. He seemed to know his stuff, but nothing he said made much sense out of that magazine article. Now maybe it was true that it cost half a million dollars to build Lulu—but most of that was written off against the experience gained. It didn't mean that Lulu was worth that much. And another thing was that developments move so swiftly in the electronics field that what is a million-dollar secret one year might be totally worthless a year or two later. My talk with Markum convinced me that the article was wrong. I suppose writers do try to be accurate, though sometimes they are more interested in sensationalism than in facts. But this time it appeared that either the writer was using out-of-date information, or else he had made a mistake on the model number. If this company really did have a secret machine, which they had developed as a prototype of a much more expensive model to come, Lulu certainly wasn't it.

"I pointed out to Kimbill that I didn't think the company would loan such a valuable machine for small operations like this contest. But he was still convinced that that was exactly what they did. He thought they were trying to test it out secretly for a series of different kinds of operation. Kimbill is only a half-smart operator. He's the kind who won't believe a big headline in the paper, but if you whisper something to him, or he comes across it as a confidential tip in some obscure place, he'll believe it. And I guess he really did have some connections in Europe which had been inquiring about this sort of thing, and he felt sure he could peddle the plans to them."

"Where was he going to get the plans?" Nelson interrupted.

"That's just it. Though most people don't know it, on these non-standard machines it's customary to keep the plans hidden in a drawer right under or inside the machine itself. That's because a repairman wouldn't be able to make repairs unless he could trace out the circuits on the blueprints. Kimbill suspected that might be the case here, and it turned out he was right.

"I took the plans last Saturday night. Kimbill had been pressuring me, but I put him off for a while, for I knew Allison was leaving town, and I didn't want to leave the *Town Crier* stuck for circulation: That's why I waited for the college vacation, when I knew you would be back, Ted. Of course, quitting the *Town Crier* was part of my plan. Kimbill would never have believed that I really intended to go in with him and his schemes—for I imagine there were others to come—as long as I kept grubbing at night work. I thought it best to let him think Mr. Dobson and I had quarreled as well. Otherwise he might believe I was simply leading him on, so that Mr. Dobson could expose him in the paper. After taking the plans I had them microfilmed. Kimbill came out a couple of times, but they weren't ready until last night. He came then, gave me the down payment he had promised—I was supposed to get the rest when he sold them—and left with the microfilms. Later I went down to the office and returned the plans. I didn't want to keep them any longer than necessary, or they might be missed.

"Now I want you to believe that I never had the slightest intention of going in with Kimbill. But look at the spot I was in. If my connection with the old black-market ring came out, it was going to be a damaging blow to my reputation. He made it clear that he wouldn't hesitate to tell, while I was in no position to expose him, for I didn't even know his real name. Then he went on to talk about my family. How were *they* going to feel about this? You could put that two ways—simply the disgrace they were going to feel, or as actual threats against them. It was then that I began to see he really had me hooked. If I went in with him—which I certainly didn't want to—I would eventually ride for a fall, because as I said before he wasn't a really shrewd operator. If I didn't, I faced exposure, and the probable loss of my job.

"I realized that it wasn't enough just to accept or reject his offer. I had to get him behind bars where he couldn't hurt anyone any more. Once that happened, I felt people would be a good deal more forgiving about my past. When he made those threats, this determination crystallized. I knew that I couldn't let him get away with that, or I'd never be rid of him. I moved my family out to the country, even though I felt they were in no danger until his scheme fell through. Just the same it was better not to have them around, in case something went wrong. Oh, I had everything figured out so I could be a real hero! As you will see, I had overlooked just one little detail.

"My plan was to have the films ready, the money change hands, and then the police move in for the arrest. Before he arrived Thursday night I phoned the police, and there I became acquainted with some of the facts of life. When I told the police about the stolen plans, they asked me what value I put upon them. I told them I was convinced they were worthless. Then the desk sergeant very patiently explained to me that you can't arrest someone for stealing unless the thing he stole has some value. If a man breaks in somewhere, you can hold him for that. If he threatens someone at gun point, you can hold him for that. But Kimbill hadn't done any of these things. He had only stolen something that was valueless!

"So that's how my scheme collapsed. Kimbill got the plans and got away, and I'm left without my part-time job that I badly need— unless I want to touch some of this filthy money, which I don't."

As he concluded his story, he looked so sad that the three boys could hardly help but sympathize with him.

"I wish I had a fairy godmother," Mr. Sawyer went on. "First I'd wish for my job back. Then I'd wish Kimbill was behind bars. Finally, I'd wish I knew what to do with this money. Too bad the day of fairy godmothers is over."

CHAPTER 16

AN ENTERTAINMENT—AND AFTER

However, the first of Mr. Sawyer's three wishes came true early Saturday morning. He came in for a conference with Mr. Dobson, and the editor agreed to hire him back. He made no criticism of Mr. Sawyer's conduct, recognizing that the circulation manager's intentions had been good, even though the results left something to be desired.

Nelson was particularly pleased by the development. "I don't suppose Mr. Dobson will be needing me next week. Work a week and loaf a week—that's my idea of a good way to spend a vacation."

With harmony restored, the office took on a feeling of good will. The return of the circulation manager meant they could get back on schedule again. In order that no one would have to work on Christmas, Mr. White hoped to get the presses moving at about one o'clock. This was not a particularly difficult thing to do, for the *Town Crier* on Tuesday morning, the day following Christmas, was going to be skimpier than usual, and Mr. Dobson had laid out as much of it as he could in advance. Mr. Sawyer intended to split his shift, doing half a night's work that Saturday night, and the remaining half early Tuesday morning.

Ted spent the morning dashing about from typewriter to telephone to files to printing room and back again. Nelson was busy, too. Besides the rest of the contributions to the Make a Wish program he had to deliver the turkeys the *Town Crier* was donating to needy families. During the noon hour he came in to report.

"Mr. Compton ran out of turkeys. He's expecting more in late this afternoon. Either he'll find someone else to deliver them, or else I'll deliver them tomorrow. I'll call him tonight after we get back from Jasonville, if it isn't too late."

Andy came in for the last of his demonstrations. For some reason it seemed to attract even more viewers than usual among the busy shoppers, possibly because many of them had not had the opportunity to see it before. Then, before he put his materials away, he showed the boys where the plans were concealed inside the machine—for of course he had been told Mr. Sawyer's story. This was Ted's and Nelson's first look inside Lulu, and they could only marvel at her extreme complexities.

"Don't ever drop a spare screw down there," Andy warned them. "You might never find it again."

"I can believe that now," Nelson agreed.

Amid a chorus of Christmas greetings, Andy left. Ted and Nelson were soon ready to leave as well. After an exchange of Christmas good wishes, the editor pressed an envelope into each of their hands.

"Your pay checks, and a little something extra for your fine work this week."

"You didn't have to—but thanks!" said Ted.

"As if college men ever needed money," said Nelson with pretended scorn.

The day was seasonably bitter, and though there was little snow on the ground, there was a strong feeling of snow in the air.

"It looks like a white Christmas," Ted predicted.

"Or maybe a black Christmas if it gets here too soon and gets all soot covered. Don't get me wrong. I'm all in favor of white Christmases, if anybody knows how to order them, but I'd just as soon not get stuck in a snowdrift with a load of kids tonight. Have you seen the list we're supposed to pick up?"

"Not yet."

"It's in the glove compartment. Take a look."

Ted did, and found that though they were picking up only four boys, they came from widely scattered communities. In fact, two of the boys lived *beyond* Jasonville, where the party was to be held, so that it would be necessary to make a circle of their route.

"And that's not all," Nelson added with foreboding. "Did you ever drive across the Ridge highway on a snowy day? The snow just seems to pile up there for some reason or other. It can be clear every place else in the state, and you'll still find heavy snow on Ridge. Maybe it's the altitude."

"Or the wind blowing up against the ridge," Ted pointed out.

"Well, whatever it is, as I said it's no place to get caught with a carload of kids. They're about ten years old, I guess. Do you think any ten-year-olds believe in Santa Claus? It seems to me they'd have to be pretty stupid to do that."

"Just the opposite," Ted contradicted, grinning. "They may be playing it real cagey."

After supper, Ted and Nelson took to the road again, ready to pick up their four charges for the Christmas entertainment.

"I wonder, Ted," Nelson remarked after a brooding silence, "what Mr. Dressier meant about finding Tony Malcolm for Mr. Gentry? If he was such a good friend of the family, he ought to know where Tony is."

"He probably does. But even if he doesn't, I don't know what we can do about it. We can't launch a country-wide search for him."

"I suppose there are some inquiries you could make—about where Tony went to school, and stuff like that. But I can't think of anything you could do that Mr. Gentry couldn't do for himself. I wonder—"

"Wonder what?" asked Ted, as Nelson paused.

"Oh, I was just thinking that before the accident Mr. Gentry was a highly successful engineer, and now he's just a department-store Santa Claus. Maybe he feels he's come down in the world, and doesn't want Tony to know about it. He might have his own kind of pride. I suppose Tony's been trying to create a life for himself, and is busy with his own affairs. But I bet he'd come running, if he knew Mr. Gentry was in trouble."

"There are a good many things I don't understand about Mr. Gentry," said Ted. "Maybe that bump on the head really *did* affect him."

Nelson suggested suddenly, "Maybe he lost his memory! How do we know he doesn't have amnesia?"

"He remembers his name, doesn't he? I thought that was the first thing an amnesia victim usually forgets."

"Someone might have told him his name, or he might have had some identification on him when he lost his memory."

"No," Ted objected, "there's that personnel card at the office. He appears to know all about his past. And Mr. Kirtland probably questioned him, too, at the store. I imagine if he had genuine amnesia we'd have known about it before this. But that bump could have affected some other part of his brain besides his memory, and that's why he's acting so queer. Well, maybe when we question him next week he'll tell us where we can find Tony, and then Tony may be able to help us work the thing out."

"Ask Lulu," Nelson suggested. "Lulu's supposed to know all the answers."

"But only if we ask the right questions. It must be our fault that we don't know the right questions to ask."

"Ask her where Tony Malcolm is and just see what she says. I'm anxious to prove she isn't any smarter than I am," he concluded with a laugh.

Ted shook his head. "If we could only put that question into the form of a mathematical equation, I'll bet Lulu could answer it. But I don't know the formula for it."

The first boy, Bruce Conquer, lived not far from Forestdale. After that there was quite a long drive to the second boy's house. Picking up the final two boys, who lived not far from each other, completed the group, and Nelson headed toward Jasonville.

The affair was held in the upstairs auditorium of some sort of meeting hall. It was gaily decorated, with a large tree at one end of the room. An amateur magician gave a short performance, and films were shown. This was followed by games, and Nelson, as a Y camp counselor, and Ted, who had assisted him part of the summer, found themselves pressed into service to help direct activities. Then refreshments were distributed and eagerly gobbled down, and a presentation of gifts followed.

"Holy smokes!" Nelson exclaimed. "Is that almost eleven o'clock? I thought this party was supposed to break up at ten."

"It was," said the director with a smile, "and it might have ended even earlier if it hadn't been for your help."

Outside with their little group, they were surprised to see how much snow had fallen. The boys were excited, but Nelson looked concerned.

"Ted, I don't like the looks of this. If there's this much snow on the ground here, how much is there going to be on the Ridge highway?"

"Can't we take some other route?"

"Sure, if we don't care whether we get home before morning. Anyway, the way it's coming down, *all* the roads are going to be bad, if we wait much longer. You see all the other cars hurrying to make tracks for home, and I don't think any of them have as far to go as we do."

"Then what do you think we'd better do?" asked Ted.

"This may sound queer, Ted, but how'd you like to take Bruce home on the bus? Meanwhile, I can deliver these other kids in the opposite direction. I don't think a bus will have much trouble. It can usually get through even where a smaller car can't."

"What about you?"

"I'll drive home if I can make it. But if I get stuck, what's the difference as long as I don't have a load of kids to worry about?"

Ted knew a decision had to be made quickly, and he gave his consent to the plan. Although he had a feeling Nelson had exaggerated the danger, still he knew they must exercise all possible care when they had other people's children in their custody.

The bus had been scheduled to get into Forestdale before midnight, but it was ten minutes after before they finally drew into the station and the passengers disembarked.

"Are we going in?" asked Bruce, as Ted paused irresolutely.

Ted didn't see much sense waiting around a cold station for Bruce's father to come, for after all he might be considerably delayed. "No," he decided, "let's go to my house and wait. We'll call your father from there."

This was agreeable to Bruce, and they started out. The snow was thick and heavy with moisture, and part of the way they found that they were the first to mar its smooth surface. Only after they had gone some distance, did Ted realize that perhaps he had made a mistake. Surely it would have been better to telephone Mr. Conquer from the station. Although all the parents had been told that the party would be late, still they might be worried. In any case, Ted could have saved ten minutes by calling there instead of waiting till they got home. However, the decision had been made, and it seemed better to continue.

Their way led past Mr. Compton's butcher shop, and Ted noticed a light in the back room. It suddenly occurred to him that this might be an opportunity to rectify his mistake. He could telephone from the shop, and meanwhile he could kill another bird with the same stone by finding out whether Mr. Compton had any more turkeys for Nelson and him to deliver On Sunday. Ted tried the front door, but it was locked.

Two doors away, an alleyway led around to the back of the row of stores. Having made up his mind to stop, Ted followed the alleyway, until he came to the rear door of Mr. Compton's shop. The door was unlocked, and they pushed in, closing it behind them. The light was coming from the room up ahead, and they made their way there.

As they entered the little room, Ted saw the door to the large freezer was open. Mr. Compton must be inside, he decided. Whoever it was must have heard them just then, and he came out of the locker. Ted stiffened, as he realized the man was not Mr. Compton unless Mr. Compton was wearing a Santa-Claus suit.

It was hard for Ted to believe that anyone except Mr. Compton had any right being there at that time of night. What was Mr. Gentry doing? Then suddenly Ted realized this was the day the contest had been held in Mr. Compton's shop. Wherever Mr. Gentry appeared, something usually turned up stolen—even when Ted had been watching. Maybe this explained it. Mr. Gentry didn't necessarily have to steal the things while he was appearing at the store in the afternoon. Indeed, it now seemed highly unlikely that he could have done so with a crowd looking on. Instead, he was merely getting the lay of the land, locating the things he wanted to steal, possibly noting any burglar alarms which might be in operation or even secretly disconnecting them. Then he came back at night to help himself to whatever he coveted. The Santa-Claus costume was helpful for anybody noticing him on the streets would have thought he was merely returning home from an entertainment. Very few if any burglars are known to disguise themselves as Santa Claus!

Santa Claus was obviously startled by their arrival, though they could not detect his facial expression through the mask. But he seemed both agitated and irresolute, as he tried to make up his mind what to do. The Santa-Claus costume would be of no help if the matter came to court. Just like any burglar, he must try to escape.

He held open the door of the cooler and motioned them inside. Ted was amazed. Surely Mr. Gentry wouldn't lock them up in the freezer, knowing it was unlikely anyone would discover them for many hours to come. But that was certainly Santa Claus's intention. He was standing close behind Bruce now, as though he might have a gun in his pocket. Ted wondered if he did, and decided the probability was good. He had little doubt that he was facing a seriously disturbed man who might have been considered merely queer until he faced exposure. Now he was frightened and desperate.

Ted hesitated for a fraction of a second. Was it better to make a stand now or not? Flesh and blood made a better object of attack than did the steel walls of the food locker. But Santa Claus was directly behind Bruce, and if he did have a gun and was prepared to use it, any attack by Ted would be foolhardy. In the freezer they faced a desperate situation, but they would still be alive, and having gained a short reprieve in time, someone might rescue them.

All these thoughts flashed through Ted's mind. He had to decide at once, for he dared not risk Bruce's life by hesitation and perhaps precipitate a rash act by this madman. All things considered, the freezer seemed the better bet for the moment.

He stepped inside. Santa Claus had Bruce by the shoulder, and shoved him in, too, so that the boy stumbled and nearly lost his balance. The door of the locker swung closed behind them. Only then did Ted recollect that no one, except Nelson, even knew they were in Forestdale, and unless Nelson returned that night, which seemed unlikely, no one would have any idea where to begin a search.

CHAPTER 17

NELSONS TROUBLES

After leaving Ted, Nelson induced the three boys with him to get back into the car. They were soon on their way, and the passengers in the back seat proved to be reasonably quiet and untroublesome, except for an occasional snicker, for they had all grown tired. Driving was not too bad, for the snow had not drifted much, nor had the roads developed a glaze as yet.

He reached the home of the first boy, and saw him up to the door. The boy's mother was glad to see him home, and thanked Nelson for his consideration.

"Is Frankie with you?" she asked. "There's no use in your taking him home tonight. He can stay here. I can phone his mother."

"It's all right with me if it's all right with everybody else," said Nelson good-naturedly, though he had not known the two boys were acquainted.

Now he had only one boy left to deliver curled up fast asleep on the back seat. Nelson tucked the blanket about him, and started out again. The snow was now falling thickly enough to cloud his vision slightly, and he drove very slowly and cautiously. He did get stuck in one drift, and had to rock the car back and forth to get out, but made it without awakening his passenger. They reached the farmhouse at last, and Nelson walked up to the door with the boy. Now with his responsibilities ended, he really felt free once more.

Nelson calculated that Ted and Bruce were probably almost to Forestdale by now. He himself headed in the same direction, determined to get as far as he could, if not all the way. He was driving along rather briskly now, still careful but without the excessive caution he exercised while he had passengers. He switched on his radio to a program of dance music, interrupted occasionally by news items. The storm was of general concern, and the announcer described the worst roads and advised caution. As he had expected, conditions on the Ridge highway mentioned were called especially bad.

Suddenly he noticed a black object ahead. A car had driven partially off the road. He drew up alongside, then got out to see if he could offer assistance. He found that the car was occupied by an older man and woman in the front seat, and a young mother holding a child in the back seat.

"Can I help you?" he volunteered.

They were glad enough to see him, but undecided just what he could do for them.

"Think you can pull me out of this drift?" the man requested.

Nelson looked doubtful. He didn't have a tow rope, and found that the driver didn't either. If they were going to get out, it meant careful maneuvering and muscle-straining exercise with the snow shovel he carried in his trunk.

"Maybe we can dig you out, but what then? Your family will be getting cold, and the driving is likely to get worse up ahead. Why don't you let me take you to some shelter for the night, and you can return to the car in the morning?"

"That's what we ought to do," the young woman agreed. "Bobby may catch cold, and he isn't over that last trouble yet."

The man looked disgruntled. For some reason he didn't like to leave the car, and Nelson began to suspect that maybe the family was short of money and he didn't want to pay for overnight lodgings. Still, it seemed the best course to Nelson, for this car was older and less equipped to battle the storm than his own.

However, for the sake of family harmony, he decided to make an effort to free the car. If they made it, they could go on and do as they pleased. If not, he could drive them somewhere. He began to direct the rescue operation. He could tell very soon that it was almost hopeless, but the man persisted. He finally suggested that Nelson line up his car behind and give him a shove. Nelson doubted the wisdom of this maneuver, but gave his consent, and the next thing he knew he, too, was stuck in the drift. With an identical predicament, digging out was now going to be twice as bad a job, and there seemed no alternative.

From this dilemma Nelson was rescued by a flashing red light and the arrival of a police car. The policeman got out and came over to inspect their operation.

"Officer, you can help us out, can't you?" the driver appealed.

"Sure, I've got a rope, and can haul you out. But I don't think you'd better do any more traveling on this road tonight. There's a little hotel about two miles back where you can put up for the night."

"I told you," said the older woman. "We should have stopped there in the first place."

After the cars were hauled out, the four people drove off.

"Where you headed?" the officer asked of Nelson.

"Trying to reach Forestdale."

"I wouldn't advise it. Things get worse the farther out you get. Say, I like those broad shoulders of yours, and there are probably other cars stuck up ahead. Want to patrol a while with me? That is, if you haven't anything better to do."

"Oh, no, I'm just out for the lark, and I always wanted to ride in a patrol car."

It was rather exciting for Nelson to listen to the police calls coming in. Of course he had occasionally heard these on shortwave radio, but now each message seemed more imperative, as he realized some of them were meant for this car and had to be acted upon. Yes, this was a thrill, and worth the trouble of spending a night on the road. They found several other cars stuck, and Nelson was glad to lend a helping hand. Finally the police car turned back.

"End of our district," the officer explained.

"Why, what place is this?"

"Don't you know where you are?"

"I know the route, but I don't know the name of the place."

"This is Lee's End."

"Lee's End!" Nelson exclaimed. "Say, I thought your voice sounded familiar. Remember me? I came with a friend to inquire about the Gentry accident a year ago."

"Why, sure, now I remember." They drove for a while in silence. Finally he said, "You know, there's a little something about that case. I didn't know whether I should say anything about it the other day. But you've helped me out, and maybe it wouldn't hurt to tell, though it's just a little brain wave of mine. I've always thought Mr. Gentry wasn't really driving that car!"

"He wasn't! Then why did he say he was?"

"I don't know whether he really said that—not at first. Because it was his car you'd assume he was driving, especially if he didn't deny it. I remember, though he seemed confused at first, he did have a little story made up later, but I was never convinced. As you recall, the other two persons were trapped in the car, but he crawled out and went for help. When I examined the wreck, it was hard for me to believe after seeing the position of the bodies that Mr. Malcolm could have been anywhere else except in the driver's seat."

"But why should he say he was driving if he wasn't?" said Nelson in amazement.

"I don't know. It seemed to be a real screwball case."

"You can say that again," said Nelson fervently.

CHAPTER 18

THE PANIC BUTTON

Don't press the panic button!

This was the phrase which shot into Ted's mind, and restrained him when he might have given way to the apparent hopelessness of their situation. If they didn't give way to sheer panic, there might be a way to overcome their problem. It was difficult and he could see no solution at the moment, but as long as there was a chance, Ted decided to do his best to make the most of the opportunities available to them.

The first thing was to keep Bruce from understanding the seriousness of their circumstances. The sudden turn of events had confused the boy. As he explained in a somewhat shaky voice:

"I thought men who were dressed in Santa-Claus suits were always nice."

"I did, too," Ted responded grimly.

But so far Bruce didn't understand, and Ted knew that the best way to keep him from understanding was to assume an attitude of unconcern. For a while, at least, Bruce could be relied upon to follow his example. Afterward, when he grew cold and hungry and tired and impatient, Ted's example would no longer be enough, but for a while it would suffice. While it did, Ted could look over their situation.

There were two lights on in the freezer, one in the front and one in the back. The walls were entirely of metal, and offered no possibility for breaking through. The door, also of metal, was equally firm, as he found by testing it with his shoulder. There was no handle on the inside, which surprised Ted. In any case, it seemed impossible to force the door from the inside.

Their problem was either to get out by themselves, or survive until help arrived. Since the difficulties of getting out seemed insurmountable, Ted turned his attention to the second possibility. Their twin enemies, he realized, were the cold and the lack of air. Which was the worst? Would it be best to exercise to keep warm, but consume more oxygen, or to rest quietly and stretch out the supply of air?

Ted looked around. The locker was a large one, and somehow Ted thought that air would be no problem for many hours to come. This wasn't like a small home refrigerator or freezer with a capacity of perhaps eight or ten cubic feet. This was a room in which a group of people could walk around, and its cubic capacity was correspondingly large. Cold was the real enemy, then. It would get them long before the air gave out.

He regarded Bruce and himself. They were warmly dressed for winter outdoor activity, but in time even their clothing would prove insufficient.

"Button up your collar, Bruce," Ted ordered.

"Why?"

"So you'll keep warm till they come and get us."

Fortunately Bruce didn't ask who was coming, or how soon, so Ted was not obliged to produce a suitable answer. For the moment he felt they had done all they could do to keep warm. Later they could undertake some light exercises, but there was no use wearing themselves out until it was necessary. So far they hadn't even begun to feel the cold.

What was their chances of rescue? Nelson hadn't been at all sure about returning to Forestdale that night, and Ted hardly dared hope that he would. But suppose he did—it was very late, and it was unlikely that he would call Ted to see how they had made out. Even if he did and the alarm went out, how would they know where to look? No one at the station had seen Ted. The bus driver might possibly remember them—or he might not—but in any case he was probably a dozen miles outside of Forestdale by this time, and it would take hours to locate him. It was the merest chance—a stray whim—that had taken Ted to the butcher shop at that hour. Surely no one would think of looking there. Even their footprints were probably snowed over or tramped out by now.

If they were to be discovered, it would probably be quite by chance. Ted remembered there might be turkeys to deliver on Sunday, and he looked over the hangers and shelves. There were no turkeys. That meant either that Mr. Compton hadn't been able to get the extra turkeys he wanted, or else he had already delivered them. With nothing more to be delivered, it was unlikely that either Mr. Compton or Nelson would come to the freezer before Tuesday morning. That would be too late—much too late for Bruce and Ted.

With the hope of an early outside rescue ruled out, Ted returned to thoughts of the cold, which ranked as their most immediate foe. This freezer was cold, but need it be so cold? He could see the coils around the sides of the walls. Could he damage those coils somehow—break them—so that the freezer would stop returning to its thermostatically controlled low temperature? Easy, now. What was in these coils? Gas of some sort—probably ammonia, which was poisonous. If he allowed the ammonia to escape, they were likely to be overcome by the fumes.

But how about the thermostat? If there was some way to interrupt the current, that would throw the thermostat out of commission, and it would no longer touch off the motors which kept the freezer cold. However, there were two other considerations. The first was what he remembered Mr. Compton had explained at the time of the power failure about how long it took a food locker to thaw out. If you just kept the door closed, he had said, chances were that the current would be on again before the meat had started to thaw out. So even if the coils were to stop freezing right now, the locker would still be too cold for Ted and Bruce as their bodies lost their natural heat. The second consideration was that if the current was interrupted, the room would be plunged into darkness, and somehow the light was one of the things that contributed to their feeling of hope. Ted didn't want to put out the light unless he had to.

So far Bruce had been holding up bravely. But he was growing tired, and his lips were beginning to tremble a little. Very soon would come questions—then inevitably tears—and finally panic.

Ted's eyes returned to that mysterious blank door that lacked a handle. Why didn't it have a handle? If it had, of course, there would have been an easy way out of their difficulty. Ted had heard of many cases where people were accidentally locked into large walk-in freezers of this kind. The designers of the locker must have had this in mind, and tried to do something about it. The door opened outward, and apparently there was some sort of gadget, worked either by compressed air or electricity, which made the door open automatically in case the latch was not fastened. This was just the opposite of some doors Ted had seen, with a similar device to insure that the door closed. The absence of a handle—why, of course, that was it. The designers didn't want a person to walk into the locker and, absent-mindedly or otherwise, pull the door closed after him. If he did, there was a possibility that the lock might jam, in spite of all the best precautions, or else that he might remain there too long and suddenly faint from the musty air. It was a clever plan by clever men, but Ted and Bruce would have been better off had they been a little less clever.

Ted wondered about that lock. It was probably a simple one, since the designers had wanted to take all possible precautions against its jamming.

Suddenly Ted recalled the night of the black-out. The failure of the power system had caused Mr. Compton to hurry back to the butcher shop. Why was it necessary for him to get down in such a hurry? He had said there wasn't any use trying to ice the meat, or anything like that. Anyhow, he had only been in the shop for about a minute. What had he done in that minute? It was tremendously important for Ted to try to figure it out. On the answer to the question might depend their chances for getting out of this ice chamber.

Something about the electricity. With the current off, something happened. Not simply the fact that the thermostat went off and the gas in the coils stopped circulating. Mr. Compton couldn't do anything about that, or at least he couldn't in the very brief time he had been in the shop. Yet he had done *something*—something that was very important.

Could it have had to do with this door? Could this door be electrically operated? A heavy door like this might work on a motor, but after examining it carefully Ted felt that this was unlikely. If not a motor, then, could it be an electromagnet? If that was it, it might mean that the door was held shut simply by means of an electromagnet. If the door was held shut simply by a weak electromagnet, he might force it by shoving his shoulder against it. He had tried it before, and it had seemed solid enough, but with this new idea in mind he tried it once more, listening carefully as he pressed. No, he distinctly heard the click of steel against steel, and knew that the door was held by a steel latch. There was little chance of his forcing that.

But the idea of an electromagnet continued to intrigue him. He had convinced himself that the door was kept closed by a magnet, but not a magnet which directly held it closed. Then what did the magnet do? Probably it held the latch down. If the current went off, the electromagnet automatically went off. Then the latch, working on a spring, snapped upward, and the compressed-air gadget would force the door to open outward! What had Mr. Compton done during that minute? He had simply closed the door of the locker and propped something against it to keep it closed until the current came back on.

Ted smiled with a feeling of great relief. Then there *was* a way out of here. If he could break the electrical circuit, the door would open by itself. But his smile faded as the more practical aspects of the problem returned to him. How could he break the circuit? There were no wires visible anywhere in the room. There were the electric lights, of course. He could unscrew one of the bulbs and insert a coin, which would blow a fuse.

Still he hesitated. His theory about the door might be completely wrong, and even if it was right it might operate on a different circuit from the electric lights. If he blew a fuse and put out the lights and the door didn't open… He knew that a considerable portion of Bruce's courage, and maybe some of his own, came from the light. To be locked up there in the dark would be a terrible thing. Worse still, from a more practical viewpoint, the darkness would put an end to any efforts they might make to help themselves. There was little they could do, with no light to see by.

Ted's decision was quickly made. There was something that might be lost by his plan, but there was much more to be gained. They certainly couldn't just stand there, if there was any way to remedy their situation. For all Ted knew, no one might come till Tuesday morning, and that would be too late.

He placed a stool under the front electric bulb. With his gloves still on, he unscrewed the bulb.

"What are you doing?" asked Bruce nervously.

"Just something I'm going to try. Stand over there, Bruce, right in front of the door."

Ted took off his glove and searched for a coin. What sort of coin? It didn't matter much. Silver and copper were both very good conductors of electricity, and a nickel contained more copper than it did nickel, anyway. The first coin he found was a dime, and he decided to start with that.

Would he get a shock? An electric shock was no fun, though it didn't seem important in view of the greater troubles facing them. Still he wanted to avoid it if he could. He recalled that his pencil had a rubber eraser on it. By balancing the dime on the end of the eraser, he might be able to insert the coin in the socket and still insulate himself from the current. He carefully balanced the coin, and gently eased it up into the socket.

Suddenly there was a spark and the remaining light went out. There was a muffled exclamation from Bruce, so that Ted wasn't sure whether or not he heard the click of the latch. He stood tensely on the stool, his pulse pounding in his ears. Then he heard the definite hum of the door swinging open!

He jumped off the stool, grabbed Bruce by the shoulder and hustled him out of the locker. Ted was jubilant. He knew their danger was ended. It was true they were not out of trouble yet, for they found the door ahead of them was locked. Apparently Santa Claus hadn't been sure the locker would hold them, and was taking no chances.

Even so, there was nothing to worry about. This was a larger room than the locker, and wasn't airtight, so they didn't have to worry about oxygen shortage. In fact, Ted could feel a draft coming in under the door. Cold was no problem, for he could close the locker door and prop something against it. Water was no problem, for they could scrape the frost off the coils, and allow it to melt in cups made out of paper. Food was no problem, for they could thaw out cold frankfurters to eat, if nothing else offered. There was no window in the room, but surely the return of daylight would bring a little light with it, and offer further possibilities. There might even be a telephone on the wall, or some instrument for battering down the wooden door which alone barred their escape.

Ted felt around and discovered a ladder, which he used to press against the locker door he had closed. He also located a table and some sort of cabinet, but no chairs. He pulled Bruce down on the floor beside him.

"It's dark in here, Ted. You won't go away and leave me, will you?"

"No, I'll be right here all the time," Ted pledged, realizing, as Bruce apparently did not, that the farthest he could go in any case was about ten feet.

"How long will it be before they come?" asked Bruce in a shaken voice.

"Not very long, I hope. But it doesn't matter, Bruce. It won't be so comfortable, but we're perfectly safe. Nothing will happen to us now."

"Will they come before Christmas?"

"I hope so. But if they don't, Christmas will wait for us. Your mom and dad will still have the tree and presents and dinner and everything waiting for you. You'll see."

Minutes passed which seemed to drag like hours. Then they heard a sound at the rear door of the building.

"Is that Santa Claus?" asked Bruce.

"I don't think so. It must be the people who have come to find us."

Then Ted heard voices, and thought he recognized Sergeant Jeffers' and Mr. Compton's. A light was turned on in the room beyond, which evidently was on a different circuit. Then the door was opened, and light flooding in caused them to blink. They quickly got to their feet.

"Is that you, Ted?" asked Jeffers. He was out of uniform, which told Ted that he must have been hastily summoned. "Everything all right?"

"Oh, yes, we're all right."

"Who's that with you?"

"Bruce Conquer. Maybe you ought to telephone his home."

"Oh, is that the Conquer boy? Why bother to telephone? I'll put him into a police car and have him home in record time."

Ted looked at his watch. To his surprise it was only ten minutes since Santa Claus had forced them into the locker—probably about five minutes spent inside the locker, and five minutes in the dark room outside. But as far as Ted's perceptions went, the experience might have lasted a lifetime.

"How did you know we were here?" he asked.

"Telephone call from Mr. Gentry. He told us all about it. I was at home, but the station called me. I routed out Mr. Compton, and here we are."

"You're sure it was Mr. Gentry who called?"

"Positive, Ted. He didn't give his name, but he hung on long enough so we were able to trace the call. It came from his home. Don't get any queer ideas that we could be wrong about that, because we aren't. I've got an officer at his home right now, making the arrest. You know, he lives just on the other side of this block. He could creep through this back alley, and never come out into the open at all. Want to come down to the station, Ted?"

"No, I guess not, if you don't need me. I'm done up."

"I understood you were locked in the freezer," said Mr. Compton, after the sergeant and Bruce had gone, "but I must have been wrong. It was only this room."

"No, we were in the freezer," and Ted quickly explained.

"Well, that was cleverly done, Ted. I suppose I could install a circuit-breaker button just inside the door. Banks even install telephones in their vaults, but a freezer seems a funny place to make a call, though it might be a good idea for some teen-agers who like to talk by the hour. But no matter what you do, Ted, no system is foolproof. If someone wants to force you in at gun point, as happened to you, he could either smash the lock so it wouldn't open, or else barricade the door in some fashion."

He understood that Ted was exhausted, and offered to take him home. Ted accepted, and the butcher, after replacing the fuse, locked up behind them. They made the short trip in silence. Mr. Compton offered to come in with Ted, but he said it wasn't necessary, and thanked him.

The lights were still on. Ted found that Mrs. Wilford had been watching a late Christmas program as she waited for him to arrive.

"Hungry, Ted?" she called to him as he kicked off his rubbers in the front hall.

"No, Mom, I don't think so."

She came in then, and saw his expression. "Why, Ted, what happened? You're so late, and your face is as white as a sheet."

He tried to smile reassuringly. "I'll tell you about it in the morning, Mom. Don't ask me to talk about it now. I'm all beat out, and I feel as if I were a million years old."

"You're not ill, are you, Ted?" she asked anxiously.

"No, I'll be all right, Mom. I guess my trouble is that I still believe in Santa Claus."

CHAPTER 19

THE REAL SANTA CLAUS

Early the next morning Sergeant Jeffers called the Wilford home. Ted was still sleeping, and Mrs. Wilford didn't wake him, but in this way she learned the details of his midnight adventures. Other calls came from Mr. Dobson and Mr. Compton, and there was an exchange of calls with Nelson's mother. Bruce's parents were also in touch with the police, so that all parties concerned were up to date before Ted came down to a very late breakfast.

As the sergeant had requested that he call back, Ted did so as soon as he had eaten. He asked if Mr. Gentry was still in custody.

"Oh, yes, he spent the night in jail. We haven't charged him with anything yet, however. We're still waiting to see how far we ought to go. That's why I wanted to talk with you."

"What has he admitted doing?" asked Ted.

"That's just it. He's admitted *everything*. That is, he told me to put everything into a confession, and he'd sign it. The trouble is, he seems to me to be confused about some of these things he did. Did you get the idea he was sort of—say, off beat?"

"I did last night. Today I don't know."

"Well, he's the queerest sort of prisoner I've ever run into. I've talked with Mr. Dobson, and so I know about all these different thefts and gifts. Now we'll have to figure out the charges. Do you want to charge him with what he did to you?"

"No, I don't think so—not as long as he made sure we'd be rescued so soon. Anyway, he'll have enough things on his head, without my adding anything. Of course I don't know anything about Mr. and Mrs. Conquer, Maybe they'll want to do something."

"They said not. They're willing to drop the whole thing. They know he's a sort of goof ball, but as long as something's going to be done about him they don't want to expose Bruce to any more trouble over it. They're just glad to have Bruce back safe and sound, and without much of a bad scare—thanks mostly to you, I guess. I better tell you that you rate pretty high in their books. They like the way you handled Bruce."

"I'm glad to hear that," said Ted with relief. "What do you want me to do about Mr. Gentry? Shall I come down to the station today and talk with him?"

"It might help matters a little if you would, Ted. You've been more or less on the inside of these thefts, so to speak. Maybe you can arrive at the truth a little more easily than I can. After all, just because he's willing to confess to anything doesn't mean we ought to charge him with things that he may not have done."

Nelson came over in the early afternoon, and they briefed each other on all that had happened since they parted.

"So I guess that settles everything," Nelson concluded.

"Maybe," said Ted more slowly.

"What do you mean, Ted? Everything's explained, isn't it? We know Mr. Gentry was in an auto accident. Either it affected him physically or mentally. Then he quit his job, and finally went to work as a Santa Claus. He got to thinking he really was Santa Claus, started stealing things, and gave them away until he got caught. That's the end. What's left?"

"Oh, I don't know. It just doesn't seem to add up to the right picture of Mr. Gentry. I can't understand him."

"Why try to understand a man who's slipped his mooring cable?"

"Somebody's got to understand him, because somebody's got to decide what to do with him. Nobody knows right now what that might be."

"Exactly what is it you don't understand about him, Ted?"

"Well, that telephone call for one thing. I can see why he would call the police and tell them about locking us up. But why should he hang on so long the call could be traced?"

"Maybe he wanted to make sure they understood him and were going to take action."

"Maybe so. But I've got to thinking. We've got a new plug-in phone, and sometimes Mom makes a call and I don't even hear her. Well, couldn't something like that have happened with Mr. Gentry's phone? It could have been his phone but someone else calling."

"He admitted making the call, Ted."

"No, he didn't admit it. He just didn't deny it."

"That's the same thing, isn't it? Anyway, I was talking to the sergeant, and he told me you thought there was something screwy about the call. But Mr. Gentry was sitting in the living room reading a book when they came to arrest him. I don't think anyone could have used his phone without his knowing it."

"Wouldn't you think he'd have been more excited about things? He'd want to know we got away all right."

"Maybe he was just covering up, pretending to be calm."

Ted considered carefully. "Another thing that comes to me is that there, in the butcher shop, Santa Claus never said a word to us. Now why didn't he?"

"Because Mr. Gentry didn't want you to recognize his voice."

"He must have known already I'd think it was he. But supposing it *wasn't* Mr. Gentry. Then Santa Claus would have to be very careful not to use his voice, or else I'd realize it wasn't Mr. Gentry!"

Nelson shook his head incredulously. "Boy, you really are serious about this, Ted, aren't you? How could it be anybody else?"

"Well, what's a Santa Claus anyway? It's just a man dressed up in a mask and Santa-Claus suit, with a pillow for his stomach if nature didn't provide him with a big enough one. That means it could be anybody. We all jumped to the conclusion it was Mr. Gentry, simply because he's the only Santa Claus we knew—because the thief seemed to be acting the way a Santa Claus might act."

Nelson was still shaking his head. "This is too much for me. This is a job for Lulu. I wish *she* could tell us the answer. But I'm sure all she'd tell us would be to recheck our data."

"Maybe she could," said Ted dreamily, "if we only asked her the right question."

"All right, brain boy, what's the question you'd like to ask her?"

"Well, of course I'd really be putting the question to Andy, and I think the question I'd like him to have Lulu answer is—how come he's got the initials A.M. tattooed on his wrist?"

"You screwy, Ted? Why shouldn't he have those initials? His name's Andrew Markum, and his initials are A.M. That all fits."

"Except for one thing. What do you think Tony Malcolm's initials are?"

"T.M., of course. No, that couldn't be right, because Tony must be a nickname. Let's see, Tony's short for—Anthony, isn't it? Or maybe Anton."

"Sure. Now do you get it?" Ted's voice showed his excitement.

"Wait a minute, Ted. Don't go too fast for me. Tony's got the same initials as Andy. So what? Probably lots of people have those same initials."

"I know. But here we have a young man named Anthony Malcolm who used to be closely associated with Mr. Gentry. Now Mr. Gentry comes to Forestdale and we find another young man with the same initials closely following him around in the background. Isn't that too much of a coincidence?"

"If he wanted to change his name, why did he pick one with the same initials?"

"People often do. It makes things easier, in case they've got their initials monogrammed on their luggage, or jewelry, or clothing, or something like that. But in Tony's case he *had* to do it, because he had that tattoo on his wrist."

"Then you think Tony and Andy are the same person, and that Tony and Mr. Gentry were in this thing together?"

"Well, let's figure that out. Was this a conspiracy? I could believe that, except that there doesn't seem to be very much profit for anybody in this deal. What good is a conspiracy like that? It seems to me only one of them is involved."

"All right, then, Ted, which one?"

"Remember Mr. Gentry came to town first, and Tony came afterward. That means it was Tony who was following Mr. Gentry, and not the other way around. Why was he following him? Evidently he didn't just come to Forestdale by chance. He planned this assignment because he wanted to come here and *pin something on Mr. Gentry!* And we know it wasn't the other way around because Mr. Gentry isn't trying to pin anything on anyone. He's still trying to cover up for Tony."

"Wow! You're beginning to convince me, Ted. But it isn't all there yet. You can't explain how Tony made that telephone call."

"Let's think about it. Suppose it was Tony that Bruce and I surprised in the butcher shop. He locked us up, then went outside, and over to Mr. Gentry's home on the other side of the block. Now what did he do? Go inside?"

"He couldn't, Ted. I don't think he could count on Mr. Gentry's covering up for him. And if Mr. Gentry knew about you being locked up, I don't think he'd have waited for the police. He'd have dashed over here and tried to get you out himself. As it was, he was quite cool and collected when the police finally got there."

"All right, then. Tony *didn't* go into Mr. Gentry's house. He stood outside and—and—Hey, I've got it! You know those little hand sets that the telephone repairmen have? They can stand outside and attach their phone to your wire. I'll bet that's what Tony did. He was calling from outside, and deliberately hung on until the call was traced to Mr. Gentry's. The police were right. The call came on Mr. Gentry's line. But it came from outside the house, not inside. He'd have to watch out for footprints there, but that mightn't be very hard, if Mr. Gentry had his sidewalk cleared."

"Then where do we go from here?"

Ted jumped up. "To the police station, of course. Let's see if we can get Santa Claus out of hock."

At the station Sergeant Jeffers was there to greet them.

"How's the prisoner?" Ted inquired cheerfully.

The sergeant shook his head. "Things are getting worse and worse. I made up a few crimes that never happened, just to see what he would say, and he confessed to them, too! Either he's playing it very, very smart or else he's all mixed up"

"Can we see him?"

"Sure."

Mr. Gentry was brought into the room and they all sat down. It was somewhat startling to see Mr. Gentry in ordinary clothes, for his voice and gestures were familiar but his appearance was strange. Ted began at once:

"You may as well tell us all about it, Mr. Gentry. We know now that it was Tony Malcolm who was doing all the stealing and trying to blame it on you."

It was the sergeant's turn to show astonishment, but Mr. Gentry simply raised his eyes and said gently: "What's your proof of that?"

"Because he had the opportunity to steal all those things, and you didn't. You couldn't have taken anything with all those people crowded around watching you. But he could. He was in those same stores, twice every day. He came in early in the morning to set up the window display, and he came back at closing time to take it down again. And if he didn't have a chance to take something then, he could come back in the evening, as he did at the butcher shop, wearing a Santa-Claus suit just in case someone caught a glimpse of him. He's a clever young man, and he'd know about burglar alarms and things."

"He couldn't have gotten into Kirtland's that way," Mr. Gentry pointed out. "He never worked there."

"No, he couldn't, but that wouldn't be so difficult, in a big store like that, with people constantly coming and going. Wait, I've got a hunch. The night of the power failure I was going into Kirtland's, when I saw Santa Claus hurrying back into the store. At the time I thought it was you, but I'll bet now it was Tony. He waited out in the parking lot till you drove off, then he himself went back into the store. An observer would think it was you coming back for something you'd forgotten. He must have done the same thing more than once, for some of the things were taken before that night."

"What about that telephone call?" demanded Jeffers.

Ted explained it, and the sergeant nodded, grimly satisfied. Mr. Gentry looked about at the faces surrounding him. He could see there was no further use in trying to protect Tony, and the best thing to do was to try to explain his actions.

"Why did he do it?" asked Ted.

"Because he hated me. You must remember he thought I killed his father and mother, the two people he loved most in the world, and that I had smashed his career as well. He dropped out of sight soon after the accident, so I never learned where he was. I didn't know he was in Forestdale, until the last few days. I suppose he knew my working hours and was careful to keep out of my way. The first thing which made me suspicious was when I was called in at Kirtland's and questioned about some thefts. Suspicions turned to certainty when Ted came in to watch me closely one afternoon. I knew then that it must be Tony who was trying to involve me somehow.

"I hadn't yet known he was the person in charge of the electronic brain, but the possibility occurred to me, and I watched his demonstration the next day from across the street, muffling my face so he wouldn't recognize me. I knew then that he was determined to hurt me in some fashion, but I didn't know when or how. Of course the arrival of the police at my home last night made most things quite clear to me. But I could still remember the warm friendship I had had with his parents—and with him—and I tried to protect him as long as I could. You must admit that he had good cause for his hatred."

"No, he didn't," Nelson broke in, shouting, "because you weren't driving the car at the time of the accident. It was Mr. Malcolm who was at the wheel."

Mr. Gentry turned toward the sergeant. "Is this off the record, sir?"

"Well, I can't lie on a police report or in court, but short of that I'll do my best to protect your secret. This accident appears to be a case which extends beyond the jurisdiction of the Forestdale police."

The elderly man turned to the boys. "And you?"

"I won't tell," Ted pledged.

"Me neither," Nelson agreed.

"Well, then, it's quite true that it was Mr. Malcolm who was driving and not I. Understand that I'm not blaming him. The accident was exactly that—an accident. It was due to the dark and the haze and the drifting snow, an unusual combination of circumstances which might have occurred to anyone. Mr. Malcolm mistook the road on a curve, just as I might have done in his place. But I felt this was a difficult matter to explain to Tony. As long as the accident had happened, it didn't seem to matter very much who was driving. The main thing I could do was to protect Tony. You can see the hatred with which he reacted toward me. It was by cultivating this hatred that he seemed to make his grief bearable. But wasn't it better for Tony to turn his hatred toward me, an outsider, instead of toward his own father? It seemed a small thing to do for his parents who had done so much for me."

"But wouldn't it be better now to let Tony know the truth?" asked Ted.

"No, I think not. I'm not a psychologist, but I believe it works something like this: by making the accident seem unnecessary, he can pretend to himself that it didn't really happen. To accept the reality of his loss would be an act of maturity for which he's not yet ready."

Ted turned to the sergeant. "Is there any reason why Mr. Gentry has to remain in custody any longer?"

"Well, not much longer, Ted. He hasn't been formally charged with anything, so I think I can arrange for his release. But the details may take an hour or so."

Ted and Nelson left the station. Mr. Gentry had thanked them, but distantly and moodily, as though he wasn't certain they had done him a favor.

"How about it, Ted?" Nelson queried. "Don't you think it would be better if we did tell, and tried to straighten things out between Mr. Gentry and Tony?"

Ted shook his head. "No, I don't think so. That's up to Mr. Gentry to decide. Maybe he's right. Tony has to grow up enough to accept the thing as an accident, no matter who was driving. Then maybe he'll be ready for Mr. Gentry's friendship again. Anyway, we promised—remember?"

"Well, maybe so, Ted. I'm not ordinarily very anxious to interfere in someone else's business. But if Mr. Gentry is really willing to do something like this for Tony, without even telling Tony what he's doing, I can only say he's a real Santa Claus."

"I guess you're right about that. I used to think a Santa Claus was just a man dressed up in a red suit. But Mr. Gentry is *for real*."

Suddenly Nelson chuckled. "This reminds me of something. I always thought that if a real Santa Claus ever appeared he'd probably end up in jail, and that's just what happened to Mr. Gentry. I guess this troubled old world isn't ready for a real Santa Claus just yet."

* * * *

Ted's brother, Ronald, arrived home in the early evening. There were decorations to be put up, and while they did this Ted told Ronald what had occurred.

"It seems to me you handled yourself pretty well in a tight spot, Ted. I don't know what I would have done in your position. I suppose I would have tried to keep a stiff upper lip, if I could, but it might not have occurred to me there was a way out. Brains can be as important as bravery in a precarious situation."

"Of course I know now that we weren't in any real danger. Not one person in a million would lock up two people in a freezer and leave them there—especially if one of them was just a little kid. Even cruel and wicked people have some kind of limit to what they'll do. If I'd only thought of that, I would have known we were almost certain to be rescued."

When they were just about finished, the doorbell rang, and Mrs. Wilford admitted Tony into the room. They were all surprised, but did their best to make him welcome.

"I came because I felt I owed you an apology, Ted," he began stiffly, "and that it would be cowardly to present it in any other way except in person. What I did to you and that little boy was inexcusable. Even though I intended to make sure you were rescued, I had no right to scare you that way. The only explanation I have to offer is that I was scared myself. I pressed the panic button."

"Exactly what did you plan to do?" asked Ted.

"Well, my plan wasn't completely clear. I had to steal something from the butcher shop, just as I'd stolen something from all the other shops—a turkey, if there was one left. Then I was going to call the police. I planned to give them a phony tip of some sort, but hang on long enough so they could trace the call, as I knew they'd do. That would lead them to Mr. Gentry, and some of the stolen stuff I'd hidden away in his garage. Of course, after you were locked in the freezer I changed my plans a little. I was scared, and ashamed that my schemes had gone to such lengths, but I still didn't intend to let Mr. Gentry off the hook."

Then the doorbell rang again, and this time it was Mr. Gentry. Evidently he had expected to find Tony there. First he talked with the others, admired the decorations, then turned to Tony, sitting with downcast eyes on the davenport.

"Tony, you want to go back to college, but haven't the money. I've got the money and want to help you. Why don't we stop this nonsense and get together the way we ought to?"

The onlookers expected Tony to make an angry retort, but apparently his recent experiences had shaken him. Instead, he replied mildly, "No, why should you?"

"For lots of reasons. Because I've known you from the cradle, because of the good times we've had together, because of the memories we share of two fine people. Because I'm a lonely old man, and you're a young man taking a lonely course through life. Why should we both go on being lonely?"

At this point the Wilfords felt it advisable to retreat to the kitchen, leaving their visitors to resolve their own problems.

"What's going to happen to Tony," Ted questioned, "I mean, because of the robberies and things?"

"I suppose there'll have to be a hearing," Ronald responded. "But I don't think anyone is going to be very harsh with a very disturbed young man who is trying to salvage his career—and juries are notoriously reluctant to convict at Christmas."

"You think they'll make it up, then?"

"I'm sure they will," said their mother warmly. "After all, this is Christmas!"

"Anyway, I don't hear any sounds of bloodshed—yet," said Ronald good-humoredly, "and that's a good sign."

CHAPTER 20

BETWEEN THE HOLIDAYS

The middle of the week found Tony busily engaged in the *Town Crier* office, running off the contest entries. Most of his work was already completed, and the rest of it was up to Lulu. An interested crowd of spectators were watching through the window, from which Ted and Nelson had scraped as much frost as possible.

"How'd you make out at the hearing?" Ted asked Tony.

"Fine, Ted. Everybody was as wonderful as they could be. When people who hardly know you express that much confidence in you, what else can you do but show a little confidence in yourself?"

"Then you're going back to college?"

"Right! At the end of January. There's going to be full restitution made, of course. Mr. Gentry will pay it, but I'm going to pay him back. And he's willing to assume responsibility for my custody. I'll miss Lulu, though—and I almost think she'll miss me. But there'll be other machines to come, even if there won't ever be another Lulu."

Ted took a small package from his pocket and handed it to Tony. The young man opened it wonderingly. It proved to be a roll of microfilm.

"Where'd you get that?" Tony demanded.

Ted looked chagrined. "I hate to tell you. I got it from Ken Kutler. You know that man Kimbill? The North Ridge police picked him up soon after he left Mr. Sawyer's Thursday night. They acted on a tip from Ken. He'd heard through the prison grapevine that a well-known confidence man had moved into the territory, and since he was wanted for crimes elsewhere, there was no trouble about the arrest. The police were surprised to find the film, and couldn't make out what it was till he finally broke down and told them."

"Well, I'm glad to get it back, even though it isn't very important," Tony remarked, pocketing the film.

"How come you didn't know about the arrest of this fellow Kimbill, Ted?" Nelson inquired.

"Because the North Ridge police were sitting on the story, covering up till Ken could get his story into print. Kimbill didn't care whether he was booked. He had to wait there in prison anyway until he could be extradited. And while he was in jail, Ken got his whole story."

"That fellow Ken Kutler's dangerous even when he's in jail," Nelson put in. "But Ken did show a lot of restraint in the way he used his story, didn't he, Ted?"

"Well, I don't know. It really wasn't a very important story, since Kimbill hadn't operated locally. Ken just used it as part of his prison series. But that part where he mentioned—oh, so casually—that this man had been caught with microfilms from the *Town Crier* office, put in big headlines, would have seemed to be something very unusual. Putting it in small type made it sound as though it was just the sort of goings-on you'd expect at the *Town Crier.* There've been some red faces around here—even Mr. Dobson's, and he usually takes these things in stride."

"Anyway, if Kimbill's arrested, Mr. Sawyer got his second wish, too."

"And his third wish," Ted added. "He didn't know what to do with the money, but now he can use it to help pay back some of the people Kimbill swindled."

Lulu seemed to be doing some unusual sputtering.

"Hold it," said Tony sharply.

"Why, what's up?" asked Nelson.

Tony smiled at the waiting crowd and held up a blackboard on which he had written:

"Lulu is about to print the names of the lucky winners."

www.ingramcontent.com/pod-product-compliance
Lightning Source LLC
Chambersburg PA
CBHW020655180626
46816CB00003B/1289